She Said It's Your Child 2

She Said It's Your Child 2

Sherene Holly Cain

www.urbanbooks.net

Urban Books, LLC
300 Farmingdale Road, N.Y.-Route 109
Farmingdale, NY 11735

She Said It's Your Child 2
Copyright © 2020 Sherene Holly Cain

ISBN 13: 978-1-893196-58-2
ISBN 10: 1-893196-58-5

First Trade Paperback Printing January 2020
Printed in the United States of America

10 9 8 7 6 5 4 3 2 1

This is a work of fiction. Any references or similarities to actual events, real people, living or dead, or to real locales are intended to give the novel a sense of reality. Any similarity in other names, characters, places, and incidents is entirely coincidental.

Distributed by Kensington Publishing Corp.
Submit Orders to:
Customer Service
400 Hahn Road
Westminster, MD 21157-4627
Phone: 1-800-733-3000
Fax: 1-800-659-2436

She Said It's Your Child 2

by

Sherene Holly Cain

Acknowledgments

All thanks, honor, and glory to God. With you, all things are possible.

To my beautiful children, Demetri, I'munique, and Shameek Stephens (grandson, Shane Stephens). Thanks for being there through good and bad times, meltdowns, pity parties, and petty situations. I love you more than I'll ever be able to express.

To my husband, my rock, my fan, my heart, Darrell Cain. Thanks for being there for me. I love you more than life.

To my sister, Angela Bennett, for all that you are. I love you to the moon and more.

To my brother, Chris Naulls, for loving my work and for encouraging me to push forward.

To my aunts, Alma Mock, Darlene Fontenot, Gloria Baker, and Deborah Baker. Cousins, Janell, Neisha, Raylecia, Raycinta, Cathy, Shonnyce, Jackie, Donnicka, Sisters Chea, Olivia, Babylisa, Brenda, and Kitten.

Thanks, Uncle Raymond, Donovan, and Duane.

Thank you, Mama Gwen Baker and Daddy Sammie Holly, for your unconditional love and all you instilled in me.

Uncle Ernest Baker, Jr., Grandpa Ernest G. Baker, Sr., and Donald Ray Stephens, RIP. You're always in my heart.

To Torica, my mentor, friend, and the world's greatest publisher.

Thanks to my Torica Tymes Presents family, especially Elle, Rae Zellous, and Chenell Parker, who continue to support my efforts and promote my books.

Acknowledgments

Margaret Flack, we are sisters of different parents, but our hearts beat the same. I love you.

Elle Welch, sis, you are a true gift for too many reasons to name.

Johnazia Gray, my lovely twin, you know how much you mean to me.

To Keyla (Keys) Anderson, my sister from another mister that has supported me since day one.

Viola King, you are such a motivating factor in my world.

To my diva, JM Hart, who is always there, no matter what, I appreciate everything from you listening to my rants, to my sleepless nights writing and trying to calm me down. You always make me feel better. So glad I have you.

Sherry Boose, when it comes to supporting, you definitely got the memo, and I appreciate you always.

Thanks, David Weaver, Cole Hart, and Torica Tymes, for the blessing.

To my sisters, Genesis Woods, Author Hope, Author P. Dotson, Jessica Wren, Latasha Shine, Laquita Cameron, Talisha Harden, and Sheena Binkley, some of the most talented writers in the game, I thank you and love you always.

Thanks to my wonderful editor, because you turn my scribbled messes into beautiful messages.

Last but not least, thanks to all my readers: Michelle, Rain, Regina, Tanya, Bijou, Keya, Tania, Sherene, Renee, Tonya, Kendra, Louanne, Christina, Liz, Tiffaney, Rita, Tamekia, Kelsi, Tremeka, Shekie, Quintana, Damon, Choum, Damon, Tee, Linda, Natasha, Latish, Donnie, Camby, Lydia, Danielle, Latoya, Yvette, Cookie, Angela, Chea, Olivia, Brenda, Keisha, Elle, Earline, Regina, and Kendra, to name a few. You're always rooting for me, and I appreciate it to the fullest. Thank you. You make it worth all the work!

Dedication

This book is dedicated to Prince.

*4 all U did and all U do, the world is better because of U.
This year, U left earth, but you'll never leave my heart.
Your legacy lives inside, and I'll remember all U taught.*

*Rest in heaven, my love, my teacher, my inspiration.
I'm still crying purple tears.*

Follow me on Facebook:
Sherene Holly Cain or Author Sherene, or
Author Sherene II

Twitter: Sherene2009

Instagram: Sherene Holly Cain

Email: enerehs2008@yahoo.com

Goodreads: Sherene Holly Cain

Amazon Central: Sherene Holly Cain

Books by Sherene Holly Cain:

Try Sleeping with A Broken Heart 1, 2, 3, and 4

The Way That I Love Him

She Said It's Your Child 1 & 2

I Can't Make You Love Me

Ring the Alarm

Cast of Characters

Darica Rogiers—A beautiful schoolteacher and interior designer who has been desperately trying to get pregnant by her husband Dolan for five years. Her desire to be a mother has made her depressed, withdrawn, and willing to do anything to have a baby.

Dolan Rogiers—An insurance agent who has been trying to get his wife Darica pregnant for five years. He confides this to his brother Nolan who eventually convinces him that using his seed would be the answer to all of their prayers.

Nolan Rogiers—Dolan's estranged brother, a surgeon with a reputation for being a playboy. He believes he has the perfect solution to his brother and sister-in-law's marital problem—donating his sperm to impregnate her with the child they want so desperately. But the brothers have a complicated relationship as it is, and it includes jealousy, fighting, and competing with each other.

Greg Rogiers—Nolan and Dolan's half brother whose mother left him in the care of their mother, Rolanda, when he was a toddler. Greg is married to a beautiful woman, Chevette, but is finding it difficult to stay faithful to her because he can't stop sleeping with the mother of his child, Rella. He often finds himself caught in the middle of his brothers' drama.

Rolanda Rogiers—Nolan and Dolan's mother. She left an abusive relationship with their father Brandon when the boys were babies and married a multimillionaire by the name of Phillip Rogiers.

Phillip Rogiers—Rolanda's husband. He adopted her two sons, Nolan and Dolan, and their half brother, Greg.

Mama C—Rolanda's mother, Nolan and Dolan's grandmother, and the matriarch of the family.

Millie—Rolanda's best friend and business partner.

Brandon—Rolanda's first love. Nolan, Dolan, and Greg's father.

April—Darica's best friend of ten years. She has a slight crush on Nolan and doesn't know he has feelings for Darica.

Nuni—Darica's close friend.

Chevette—Greg's wife and Darica's close friend. She's been trying to get pregnant since she found out he's having an affair with the mother of his child. Chevette believes a baby will bring her and her husband closer.

Evette—She has been sleeping with Nolan for a year, but in his opinion, they're not in a relationship. She knows he has feelings for Darica and is determined to get her out of the way.

Carlena—Dolan's ex and high school sweetheart. She's slept with him twice since he's been married but continues to hold on to the hope that he will leave Darica to be with her. She will go to any length—including murder—to get her man.

Miko—Dolan's friend from high school who had fallen in love with him until their friendship ended because of her promiscuity. She's trying to win him over again.

Dr. Ross—Miko's psychiatrist.

Payne—A man who is in love with Evette.

Litha—A private detective Nolan initially hired to keep tabs on Darica.

Nurse Ratchet/Lala—An undercover cop on assignment at Lake Hospital.

Detective Hughes—The detective investigating the disappearance of three women affiliated with Nolan.

Mina—One of Nolan's former lovers.

Essence—A prostitute.

Previously

Evette

When I walked into the house and heard Dolan making the announcement, I knew Nolan had finally done the unthinkable. This Darica bitch was pregnant, and if Nolan was the father, I knew she had to go. All I could think about was the fact he always wore condoms and kept pulling out so that I couldn't get pregnant, and here *she* was walking around like getting pregnant by him was the thing to do.

The fucked-up part about it was that she was Dolan's wife. I didn't know exactly what I was going to do about any of this, but I was sure I would hurt her real badly if she said it was Nolan's child.

Carlena

After all the years I had put into getting Dolan back, he went and married that bitch and tried to give her a baby. He wouldn't even let me get off birth control.

When I saw them walk into that clinic looking for a donor, I almost went ballistic. I felt that if he had any sense, he would've made a U-turn and run for the nearest exit when he saw me. I knew plenty of doctors—ones who would tell him he had a low sperm count and give him medicine to make it appear to be true. I didn't count on Nolan helping them but making myself available as a volunteer counselor so that I could destroy the samples every time Nolan submitted them was an ingenious backup plan.

I knew the only way Darica could be pregnant was if Dolan stopped taking that medication or if she cheated with another man. And since I had no way of being sure, I was going to have to get rid of the bitch the best way I knew how.

Darica

The look on Carlena's face when she came from out of nowhere was nothing like the sweet expression I was used to. When she shoved me in the closet, wound duct tape around my mouth and arms, and put a sharp knife into my back, I was more than shocked.

Carlena

"Okay, bitch. I'm going to talk, and you're going to listen. If you make one move and alert anyone that we're in here, I'm going to fillet your ass. Do you understand?" She nodded, knowing I meant business. "Good girl. Now, let me bring you up to speed. I've been fucking Dolan off and on for years." I paused for effect and watched her reaction. She shook her head, and I saw tears in her eyes. Then I went on with my story. "*I* was his first love, so that shows you where you are on the totem pole. That baby he says he wants so badly means nothing to him. He's just playing you until he can make the divorce happen. Since you are technically in the way, I'm going to help him along. We already know he can't give you a baby, so it's safe to say that you fucked someone else to get it. Am I correct?"

She gave me the look of death, so I kept on talking. "It's fine if you don't want to talk, but let me warn you that I *know* the treatments didn't work. You can't tell that to your husband, now, can you? It seems to me like the only thing left for you to do is leave, so Dolan and I can be happy." She shook her head "no" at that point, and I knew what I had to do.

Darica

I couldn't believe Dolan betrayed me with such a crazy bitch, but when I felt the sharp knife plunge into my stomach, I knew she was serious. The wound was so deep that, in a matter of seconds, I was too weak to move. I couldn't call out with the duct tape on my mouth, so I resolved myself to the fact that I would bleed out and feared for the life of my unborn child more than my own.

I listened to Dolan and Nolan frantically looking for me and making phone calls from the other side of the door. They had called the police and formed search parties to look for me, and I was right there under their noses. I imagined the expression on their faces when I was finally found dead in the closet. I also thought about the humiliation they would suffer when the true story was revealed.

Flashbacks of my childhood and wedding, flashbacks of Mama, Daddy, Ben, April, Nuni, Nolan, Dolan, and my unborn child invaded my thoughts as I drifted into darkness, and, suddenly, I hated myself for every choice I had made, including coming to this god-forsaken party.

Dolan

I thought the police would never arrive, so I was somewhat relieved when a detective finally came in. We had been looking for Darica in the huge house, and when we didn't find her, we didn't know what to think. April was frantic, my mother was hyperventilating, and everyone else was so nervous, they could barely move.

"Hello, Mr. Rogiers, I'm Detective Hughes," he addressed my brother.

"Are you here about my wife?" I asked.

"No. I'm here to question Nolan Rogiers about the disappearance of Sheila Carter, Essence Jackson, and Wilhemina Jones, a coworker, a prostitute, and a friend of his that were all last seen with him, all having relations with him, and all missing."

Chapter One

Carlena

It wasn't easy scrambling around in that small-ass closet trying to put on the oversized maid's uniform I found. There were a half-dozen brooms and mops, twenty bottles of cleaning supplies, fifteen staff uniforms falling off the hangers, and Darica was on the floor bleeding like a stuck pig. I knew it was only a matter of time before the red shower would squirt me, and then, I would truly be busted. By the time I peeked out to see if the coast was clear, people were already calling her name. I ran down the hall so fast, I almost tripped and cracked my head.

"Get it together," I scolded myself while I looked down to make sure I was presentable enough to pass myself off as the help. There was blood on the edge of my garment. It must have splattered when I was stabbing her.

"Shiiit!" I accidentally yelled. I felt my heart pound against my chest, and it got even wilder when Nolan rounded the corner, and I almost knocked him down. I thought he was going to recognize me, but he was so engrossed in finding her, he breezed right past. I always knew he had a soft spot for the bitch, but now it was blatantly obvious he was looking for her for his own selfish reasons. Unfortunately for him, the only thing he'd find was a corpse.

I darted through the kitchen, almost falling flat on my face again on some butter that was on the floor. I miraculously made it out the back exit where a food truck was waiting to be unloaded. I jumped in, found a spot all the way in the rear, and hoped like hell I wouldn't be discovered by the workers and have to pay them off. I thought about getting in the driver's seat and tearing down the road, but the consequences of the truck being reported stolen outweighed my options. Besides, I wouldn't be any good to Dolan if I were caught. The driver closed the door, and I heard the latch click, his feet shuffle toward the front of the truck, and the motor come to life. Lucky for me, he only took half the food into the Rogiers's residence, and the food I was hiding behind was scheduled for another location.

When the vehicle stopped in front of a restaurant, and the driver opened the doors and went to confirm his delivery, I jumped out, ran in the opposite direction, and called a cab from a phone I borrowed from an elderly lady. When I got home, I took off the uniform, yanked off the party dress I had on under it, burned the clothes, took a shower, and threw on a blouse and a pair of jeans. It was a good thing I rented a car to get to the party. I called the rental company to buy me some time to have someone pick it up from their house.

"Luxury Rentals," the receptionist sang.

"My reservation number is MQ797438J. I'm going to be keeping the car for another day."

"Okay, ma'am. That won't be a problem. Thanks for calling."

"You're welcome, love."

I took a few deep breaths and forced my breathing to return to normal. I was nervous as a tick, and my hands were still trembling as I grabbed the keys to my car and headed to the hospital. My mind started racing, hoping that bitch was dead. I couldn't wait to start my life with Dolan.

Darica

After Carlena's crazy ass stabbed me like I was a piece of Styrofoam instead of a human being, I watched the scary bitch creep out of the closet and quietly close the door. I listened to her footsteps grow faint, and another set come closer, hoping they were coming to help me. Whoever it was walked right past the closet and took away any hope that Carlena would pay for what she did or even be questioned about whether she saw me. She looked so desperate; I almost felt sorry for her. I couldn't believe she was trying to kill me over a man I probably would've handed over to her on a platter. Hell, all I wanted to do was live long enough to see my baby. I cringed at the thought of her getting my family and wondered how I missed all the signs, the ones that were screaming at me if only I'd taken the time to listen. They were most definitely there, but, unfortunately, it was too late to go back.

I had a dream that Dolan came into the cold dark closet and rescued me, and it seemed so real. But now, I know that couldn't be true because Dolan was nowhere in sight, and I was taking tiny breaths because deep ones made the blood gush out harder. My mind kept racing with thoughts of wanting to live but feeling so weak that I wanted to die. My heart was filled with anger, thinking only of my husband and a lover who couldn't live without him, thinking only of the family I worked so hard to obtain, thinking of my child who would never get to see the light of day. I wanted to kill that bitch with a wrath ten times worse than what she unleashed on me, but I couldn't even muster up enough strength to kick the door, stand up, or make noise to alert anyone I was here. Somewhere along the way, I gave up my fight, and

I assured myself that I was definitely going to die in that closet.

My body went into shock. I stopped feeling pain at all. My mind went through trips, flashbacks, slips of consciousness, or maybe it was my brain simply passing the time until I drew my last breath.

The light coming from the far end of the closet startled me. At first, I thought someone was coming to rescue me, and I wondered why they just didn't open the door, but then the light gave way to a tunnel, and when I got to the end of it, I saw people I knew, folks I hadn't seen in ages. I thought it was a dream. I'd heard people on TV talk about "the infamous white light" a million times, and I'd shake my head in disbelief, thinking this was a bunch of bull because there was no way that crap was real. I believed we all faded into the woodwork of the universe when we died. But what I was looking at right now was the truth, and thank God I was getting a chance to experience it.

My grandmother, who died of a heart attack a decade ago, stepped forward. Directly behind her was my friend from elementary school who got hit by a truck and my old coworker, who was a victim of a drive-by. They were waiting for me, and I extended my arms to embrace them. I waited for them to grab me too. My grandmother took another step, but instead of reaching her arms around my body to engulf me with her love, she put up the palm of her hand and said, "Darica, it's not your time. Go back to that man. He needs you."

"What man, Grandma, and how the heck am I going back to anybody when there's no way out of this freaking closet?" I asked curiously . . . just as a sharp pain ripped through me. It felt like someone dug in my back with a sword and unrelentingly pushed it all the way to the center of my throat. I wanted to scream, but no words came out.

"Baby, I will see you later," was all she said as she faded away, leaving me to endure the pain and wonder who the man was that she was referring to. Damn. She could have given a bitch a clue.

Nolan

"I'm sure you heard what I said, Mr. Rogiers," Detective Hughes spat. Every time the son of a bitch looked at me, I knew he thought I was guilty. He got all up in my face like he was about to kiss me, and his breath smelled worse than a bucket of dirty chitterlings. I moved back to get him out of my personal space because he apparently didn't know my nose was about to shut down.

"If the crime was having sex with them, I'm guilty as sin, but if you're talking about anything else, you can miss me with that. I've never killed anybody in my life."

"You're the one who assumed they're dead. I never said that, so I *am* going to need you to come down to the station."

"Am I under arrest?"

"No, but I think you can shed some light on their disappearances, and if nothing else, we can rule you out as a suspect."

"A suspect for what?"

"Oh, hell no! I'm calling Daddy's attorney, baby!" Evette yelled out of the blue.

I barely even noticed she was there until I heard her voice. I had told her it was over, thought I made a clean break, but I guess she didn't get the memo we were done. Besides, the last thing I needed was her ass all up in my business. I didn't trust her ass.

"That won't be necessary," I declined. I planned to cooperate because I knew they wouldn't find anything on me, but I wasn't going anywhere until I found Darica.

"We're having a family crisis right now, but I'll be at the station in a few hours," I pulled the detective to the side and said.

"Thank you, Mr. Rogiers. I'll try not to take up too much of your time. Here's my card. Let me know when you're on your way."

"OK," I said as I made my way over to my mother, stepfather, and the few guests who were still present. The rest of the guests were talking about making flyers and whatnot. I saw another detective talking to Dolan.

"What the hell is going on?" my father yelled.

"I hope this doesn't have anything to do with you," my mother spat.

"Why are you talking to me like that, Mom?"

"Can you blame me? Every time I look around, something crazy is happening, and it *always* points to you."

"But you're yelling at me like it's all my fault, or I started it or something. You must've forgotten about Greg and all his baby mama drama. Dolan ain't no saint either."

"Phillip, if you don't get your son, I swear—"

"I'll handle this baby," Phillip interrupted.

"I'll be back, Pops. I have to go to the restroom," I said. I was mad as hell about the accusation and needed to get away from them before I said something out of pocket. I also had too much to drink, and if I didn't go to the bathroom soon, my bladder was about to bust. I handled my business, washed my hands with hot, soapy water, then turned on the cold to splash on my face. I thought about my track record. What if this were my fault? I would never forgive myself if something happened to Darica because of me. I took a few deep breaths, opened the bathroom door, and looked out to make sure my parents were nowhere in sight.

Maybe I was focusing my attention in the wrong direction. After all, Dolan had his skeletons too. He didn't even know that on his wedding day, I put out a major fire. Carlena's ass was packing heat, and she was about to bring the whole house down. She had the gun pointed in Darica's direction when I grabbed her from behind and yanked her backward.

"Whoa, sweetheart. You don't want to do that. Let me have the gun," I said as I pushed her into a waiting room on the side of the church. The crazy bitch was strong as an ox and determined as hell to put a hole in somebody.

"Let me go," she said.

"Aaaah!" She hit me in the groin like a sumo wrestler.

"I'm not going to let her ride off into the sunset with my husband."

"He's married to you?" I managed to belt out when I recovered.

"No, but he could be. I love him. I have to stop this wedding."

"You want to tell him that from prison? Because that's where you'll be if you pop anyone today. Now, give me the gun." She did as she was told and started crying. I took the bullets out, wiped the sweat off my face, and put the gun in my suitcoat. She couldn't do much damage without a weapon, but I escorted her out, just to be sure.

"Whew," I sighed as I watched her walk out of the church in defeat. I had come in because I thought it was finally time for Dolan to come clean, but the battle with Carlena made me late. By the time I got in the church, everyone was seated, and Darica was heading down the aisle. Shit was awkward as hell. I was out of breath, sweaty, and tongue-tied. I must have looked like a psychopath by the time Darica saw me.

Dolan knew good and damn well he should've been honest with his fiancée. But I knew exactly how he felt because the truth of the matter was, I was no better. I had my own battles, and, back then, I was a whole different man. Time *had* made me wiser; yet, it was time that I was quickly running out of.

I decided to cut through the dining area to avoid everybody, and that brought me back to the problem at hand. As I was making my way down the hallway, I saw what looked like blood on the floor. It was seeping out of a small broom closet. I opened the door and couldn't believe my eyes. Darica was sprawled on the floor, unconscious in a pool of blood. She was duct taped like a mummy with holes in her body, and I had never before seen stab wounds like them. I felt for a pulse and got one, found clothing and other accessories in the closet to slow the bleeding, and went right into saving her life. Now that I found her, I didn't want to take her to some noisy hospital; I wanted to whisk her away to my new house. I had everything I needed to work on her, including bandages, needles, medications, and IVs. But there was no way in hell I was going to get her out of my parents' house undetected.

I thought about sewing her up, but the wound seemed too deep, and I had no way of knowing of internal damage. That would be too drastic a move that might do her more harm than good. I had to get her to the hospital if I was ever going to stop the bleeding and run the necessary tests.

"I'm sorry, baby," I whispered. "I don't know who did this to you but trust and believe, I'm going to take care of everything. I wish it were me instead of you. I guess I'll have to break it to everybody. Brace yourself for the confusion. Stay strong. I love you." She wasn't responding, but I knew she heard me. I gave her a final kiss on the lips and called the ambulance.

"911, what's your emergency?"

"I have a stab victim at 12814 Crestview Estates. Hurry," I demanded.

"Help is on the way, sir. Can you tell me what happened?"

"I don't know. I found a woman inside a closet injured. I'm a doctor. By the time I got to her, she was unconscious. I've stabilized her, but she needs medical attention. Get someone here fast."

Dolan

I barricaded myself in a guest room, pulled out my bottle, gulped down as much whiskey as my mouth could hold, and waited to feel the effects of the alcohol. My phone was ringing off the hook, but I ignored it. I needed to gather my thoughts and process this. How the hell was my wife missing on her birthday? I planned this shit for weeks, and there was no reason why it would be anything but perfect. Right about now, we should be cuddling in front of the fireplace while I tell her about the new business venture I was about to partake in. We should be celebrating the fact we finally got the baby we waited for so long in her stomach and the end of our financial troubles. I felt helpless, sitting idle, while Darica was God knows where. Maybe she was with some lunatic, and I hoped Carlena or my brother wasn't one of them. I took a few more swigs and pondered my only two choices. I could sit here and wallow in self-pity, or I could get out there and look for my wife.

The answer was a no-brainer. I jumped up, grabbed my keys, and lifted my coat when I looked down at my phone and saw it light up again. I had missed two calls from Nolan, but he was making a third attempt. *Aw, hell. What does this fool want?* I thought, although I shouldn't have been surprised that he was calling me, instead of walking up to me to say what he had to say. His coward ass was probably on some bullshit and scared to face me. I thought about letting the call go to voicemail just to be petty, but I was actually anxious to hear him out.

"Yeah," I blurted into the phone.

"I found Darica."

"*What?*"

"She's in the broom closet in the east wing. It's not pretty."

I disconnected the call in the middle of his sentence, sprinted through the house, and made it to the east corridor before I took my next breath. My heart was beating so fast that it felt like it was going to burst through my chest. At that moment, I wished I would have stayed on the phone to listen to the rest of his spiel because I wasn't sure what was about to go down.

I saw my wife sprawled on the floor before I reached the doorway, stopped dead in my tracks, and pushed Nolan out of the way. My legs felt weak, and I fell to my knees on the floor in a pool of her blood.

"Oh my God!" I said so loud to her still form, everyone in the house heard me. My body collapsed, and it felt like all my limbs gave out. I checked for a heartbeat and a pulse but felt nothing, maybe because I was too worked up to feel anything. I took her hands in mine and kissed them. "Hold on, baby. Help is on the way," I promised, almost choking on my own words because the paramedics were nowhere in sight.

Suddenly, they burst in the door and ran to where we were. I was instantly standing in the hallway while they worked on her, hooked her up to machines, and placed her on a gurney.

"She'll be going to Lake Hospital. Are you riding with us?" one of them asked.

"Of course," I said. Everybody started grabbing purses, coats, and keys and headed out the door to get to the hospital like it was a race.

I must've looked a hot mess with blood and dirt all over my clothes and sweat all over my face, not to mention I smelled like someone poured alcohol on me. I'd never been so scared in my life. But now, I was wondering if my wife was going to live. On our wedding day, when we said "'til death do us part," I never thought it would be this soon. We were both on cloud nine that day, and I never thought anything would threaten our happiness.

Right now, as I was running after the gurney that held my wife, the reality of the situation brought me back to the present. Regardless of how we started, this was where the wheels of destiny had us right now. I made a vow right then and there that if my wife survived, I would tell her the truth about everything for the rest of our lives, no matter what.

The paramedics didn't allow people to ride in the back like you see on TV, so I was forced to watch from the passenger seat as they worked on Darica. I saw her give up a few times, but I begged her to stay with me. I knew she heard me when I saw her fighting for our family, and I held on to the glimmer of hope that we would definitely have one.

April

I was doing ninety miles an hour, running every light in the city, and it still felt like the longest ride I ever took.

"Please, God," I prayed, "I'll do anything if you let me see Darica again."

"Slow down, *chica!* You're scaring me!" Chevette yelled from the passenger seat, reminding me I wasn't in the car by myself.

"Sorry. I'm just trying to get there," I explained.

"I want to get there too, but it won't help if we have an accident," she reasoned.

"My bestie tried to fool me, but it didn't take a rocket scientist to see she was going through a lot, scared, nervous, and a million miles away whenever we talked. I knew all about her run-in with the monster at the club, her birthday curse, and her attack at the crack house, but none of those things ever rattled her like this."

"I don't understand any of that, but I'm sure you'll fill me in later. When she jumped up and ran to Nebraska for a month talking about she missed Nuni and needed a change of scenery, that's what did it for me."

"Who does that?"

"A desperate woman, for sure. I thought everything was okay after that. Do you think she got into some trouble, and that's why she was acting so strangely?"

"I don't know. I planned to talk to her after the party, but I never got a chance because there was always something standing in the way. I had to admit that, after everything that went on, I never dreamed something this crazy would happen. My sister is the sweetest thing on God's green earth, and I can't think of anybody who would want to hurt her like this. One thing for sure, when I find out, the fool is getting their ass beat."

"I'm with you."

I turned into the hospital parking lot on two wheels and ran in there, just as they wheeled her in, feeling helpless as I watched her little body curled up in a ball. I wasn't used to seeing her like this, and it was extremely hard. After chasing the gurney for what felt like an eternity, I grabbed her hand.

"I'm here, sis. You gotta fight."

"You have to go," the hospital staff said as they pushed me out of the way. I ended up in the hallway by myself.

Dolan, Rolanda, Phillip, Nuni, Chevette, Darica's mother, and I took a seat in the waiting room, while Darica was wheeled into the operating room. We were all on pins and needles and couldn't speak. Nobody wanted to say the wrong thing. I felt sorry for Dolan as he sat there in tears, waiting for an update on his wife. They had gone through so much; it didn't seem fair for them to suffer anymore. It was enough they had to rely on his brother to donate sperm so they could get pregnant, but dealing with his ex-girlfriend accusing him of cheating was another battle they could do without. Even after the truth came out, Darica and Dolan still seemed to be having problems reconnecting. I knew they wanted to grow old together, among other plans they made for their life, and I said a silent prayer for them.

"Family of Darica Rogiers," a doctor called out.

"Yes," we all said.

"Hello. I'm Dr. Jones," he said. "Darica has several deep puncture wounds in her stomach, back, and side. There's damage to some internal organs, and she's lost a lot of blood. We're trying to stabilize her with medications until we know if we can go in and operate. We're doing everything in our power to help her. I'll keep you posted."

"Will my wife be okay?" Dolan asked.

"She seems to be responding to treatment, but at this point, we don't know much. I'm sorry. I wish I could assure you, but right now, that's all I can tell you. We just have to wait it out."

"Hello, Doctor," Phillip said.

"Hi," Dr. Jones answered.

"I'm Phillip Rogiers. I'm sure you recognize my name by the generous donations I supply to this hospital."

"Yes. I know who you are, sir."

"Listen, that's my daughter-in-law in there. I want you to do everything in your power to save her life."

"I understand, and we most definitely will try."

"Don't *try*. *Succeed*."

"Yes, sir. Please excuse me," Dr. Jones said as he made a quick exit.

Chapter Two

Nolan

All I could think about was Darica in the hospital, and me stuck over here with a dumb-ass detective that didn't know shit. But I knew if I didn't get him off my back, things would only get worse for me. He was asking the same questions over and over, and the whole time we were talking, he didn't bother to grab one piece of gum. His dragon breath was all in my face, and it was pissing me off.

"When was the last time you saw Essence?"

"Who?"

"The prostitute."

"I told you it was a week ago."

"You said you *think* it was a week ago. What was the last thing she said to you?"

"The same thing people always say when they leave . . . goodbye."

"Now you're being a smart-ass. Did you see where she was headed?"

"Her car was still parked when I left. I had somewhere to go."

"Where did you go?"

"I went to see my sister-in-law in Nebraska."

"Can she corroborate your story?"

"No. She wasn't home. I talked to a friend of hers. She can tell you I was there."

"What is this friend's name?"

"Ari. I have her phone number right here."

"How about your coworker?"

"The last time I saw Sheila was in the lunch room at the hospital."

"Miss Mina?" he asked.

"She contacted me a few weeks ago to try to hook up with me."

"What did you tell her?"

"I told her I wanted nothing to do with her, that I had moved on."

"So, you guys broke up?"

"I just told you we were never together."

"She was cool with that?"

"No, but she had no choice. Look, are we almost done because I have somewhere I need to go?"

"Like?"

"I need to get to the hospital to see my sister-in-law."

"So, you followed your sister-in-law to Nebraska? You must really be close," he pried. I shook my head at him. "Thank you for your time. We'll be in touch if we need you," he said.

"You're welcome," I told him as I got up to make my exit. I truly felt sorry for all three women and hoped he would find them alive and well.

The twenty-mile drive to the hospital gave me plenty of time to think about all the events that occurred in the past month. My main concern was Darica and what she was going through. I wondered what maniac would come into my parents' house and stab her like that. I came up with a blank. I was halfway to the hospital when I got a call from Evette. Out of instinct, I ignored the call, but she kept hitting redial until she finally filled up my mailbox with her messages. When I listened to them, I hardly recognized her voice. She sounded frantic.

"Nolan, I have something to tell you," she said. Against my better judgment, I called her back.

"This better be good, Evette."

"It is," she said.

"What is it?"

"You need to come to my house. I have to tell you this in person."

"If this is some bullshit, I swear—"

"It's not. I promise," she cut me off to say.

"I'm on my way," I told her.

She was waiting at the entrance when I arrived and pounced on me the minute I walked in. She grabbed my neck, wrapped her legs around my waist, and tried to force her tongue in my mouth. I pried her hands from around me, but that only made her grip me tighter.

"I thought this was an emergency."

"It is."

"What is it?"

"I'm pregnant."

"Yeah, and I'm the king of England."

"You have to believe me, baby."

"I'll believe a pregnancy test and some DNA results, in that order."

"I'll get them to you as soon as I can."

"You do that."

"Nolan?"

"What?" I spat.

"I'm aching for you."

"Darica is in the hospital dying, and all you can think about is sex?"

"I was wondering how long it would take for you to mention her. Baby, that woman doesn't give a shit about you. She's married. I've been with you from day one. I love you, and I'm carrying your child. We need to make it official."

"The only thing that's official is that you're crazy, and if you keep fucking with me, I'm going to call the Pet team."

"Y-y-you don't mean that."

"Every word."

"I don't need a psychological evaluation. I need you. Be my husband, and I'll make you the happiest man in the world."

"Hell no. Get off me!" I demanded as I looked into her eyes. I saw something in them, a level of crazy I'd never seen before. "I wouldn't be surprised if *you* were the one that stabbed her."

"Is that what happened to her?"

"Like you don't know."

"Is she okay?"

"I have to go."

"To her?"

"Yes," I said as I left her standing there with her mouth hanging open and started for the door. I was about to walk out when I heard her cock the hammer on the gun. "You going to kill me now?"

"No. But I will make your life hell if I don't get what I want."

"What is that?"

"I just want you to stay with me tonight."

I knew that translated to "I want you to knock my back out tonight." But the only thing I could think about was Darica dying while I was here with this silly woman.

"I wouldn't touch you with a ten-foot pole, let alone a ten-inch one. What part of 'done' don't you understand?" I walked out before she could answer and ignored her screams for me to come back.

I tried calling April and Dolan, but they didn't answer. I knew they were just as broken up as I was, but I wanted to know the status just like everybody else. I walked into the hospital and observed them from a distance. Dolan was livid. He was wringing his hands and sweating bullets. April was a basket case. She didn't know what to do. Her mother and Chevette were crying. Nuni was pacing the floor. He sat down several times, bolted up, down, and back up again.

"I can't take this anymore," he said. "My girlfriend is not going to die. She's going to make it, you hear me? I don't know what's going on, but whatever it is, we'll get through it."

"He's right," Mama C chimed in. "I think we need to join hands in prayer because it's going to take more than just hope. It's going to take divine intervention. That woman in there is fighting for her life, and we need to make sure she keeps it," she said as she began praying in a hushed tone. I bowed my head too.

After we prayed, I took a walk through the hospital, my place of business. I looked at Darica's chart. She was in a lot of distress, serious internal damage, and swelling. They were using medications to control it, and they planned to operate. Carlena came out of her office. I hadn't seen her in the hospital in so long; I thought she didn't work there anymore. She had a smirk on her face like she knew something. I didn't trust her sneaky ass and felt like she shouldn't be allowed to work at both the hospital and the clinic. But I guess it wasn't my place to interfere with people's livelihood. I didn't say a word to her as I headed straight to the operating room.

"Who's going to do the procedure?" I asked.

"Dr. Jones," the nurse said.

Oh no. Not him, I thought to myself. The last operation he performed was so botched up, the patient barely survived. He had made incisions in some places that didn't need them and failed to put stitches in others. I saw Doc Jones washing up and preparing for the procedure. He had alcohol on his breath and looked like he was about to fall out any minute. I wasn't against a few beers on my days off, but it was a no-no if I even thought a patient was going under my knife. This guy was about 70 years old and was known to drink hard liquor. He looked extremely nervous and somewhat confused, almost like he wasn't sure if he could handle it.

I stood there on pins and needles watching his every move before walking in, making a few suggestions, and telling him not to worry. He assured me he was okay, so I walked back out. I didn't get two feet away before he dropped the scalpel twice, rubbed his eyes like he couldn't see, made an unsuccessful attempt to stop his hands from shaking, and began to wipe beads of sweat from off his face. They should've asked Nurse Love to operate because she had a better chance of saving her.

I put on some clean scrubs, threw on my white coat, washed my hands, ran in, and whispered to him that I was taking over. He looked like he wanted to protest, but the nurse and anesthesiologist gave him a pleading look and nodded in agreement. They didn't know this patient from a can of paint, but they didn't want to watch another young woman die either.

Evette

Nolan had me all the way fucked up, and if I didn't love the hell out of his ass, I would definitely hate his guts. He better be happy as hell I wasn't his enemy. I was running out of options, and it was getting on my nerves. The life I wanted was long overdue, and it was more embarrassing as the months dragged on.

I poured myself a drink and made my way to the den when I noticed the fireplace was going. I knew I didn't start it because I had barely made it home. I went over to investigate and saw Payne lying in front of it on the rug, the bearskin rug where Nolan and I used to make love. The man was buck naked, and I couldn't lie, looking sexy as sin. He looked so much like Nolan, it was scary.

"Surprise!" he yelled. I couldn't contain the frown on my face, and he knew I was in a bad mood.

"Damn, Payne. You scared the shit out of me. What are you doing in my house?"

"So, that was the infamous Nolan, the man who has your heart? Looks like you don't have his," he answered, fully ignoring my question.

I made a mental note to beef up my security and change my locks.

"I didn't call for you, so put your clothes back on and get out of here."

"You wasn't saying that when I was deep in them guts."

"You know what time it is. You can dress up, cut your hair, and trim your beard, but at the end of the day, you'll *never* be him."

"But I'm a damn good replacement. I studied your man like I was writing a thesis on him. But I have to admit, seeing him up close and personal made me jealous."

"When they made Nolan, they broke the mold."

"Maybe so, but I know you have feelings for me. The way I suck that clit and beat that cat, there's no way you're walking away that easy. You need to stop dreaming and realize *I'm* the man for you."

"You're the man for Daddy."

"What? I don't swing that way."

"I didn't say you did, idiot. I meant that Daddy wants me to be with you."

"Your daddy is a smart man."

"My daddy doesn't run my life."

"Read my lips, Evette. Nolan doesn't want you. I came over because I missed you. You been acting like a stranger.

Now, come over here and let me lick you; I mean, lick your wounds like I always do."

Payne knew I wouldn't protest, especially after seeing Nolan's fine ass, so he undressed me and laid me down on the rug.

"Not here," I said. "On the couch."

"Whatever you say, Queen."

After I got rid of Payne, I took a shower and changed clothes. I was still pissed off at Nolan, and the sad part about it was I didn't know what ticked me off the most. Was it the fact that he didn't believe I was pregnant because he felt I couldn't or shouldn't be, or the fact that he'd never thought enough of me to bring me around his family. I begged to meet his mother so many times, it was ridiculous. But my pleas for him to grant me that one of many wishes always fell on deaf ears.

It seemed like only yesterday that I decided to pay Rolanda a visit on my own.

I took the drive to their estate via the hood and noticed the streets were full of young women who had two or three babies trailing behind them. That let me know I was long overdue. I thought of the last conversation with Payne.

"It's a shame that the same man who would deny your child would welcome another woman's kid with open arms, and the man you have no regard for would die for you to have a baby by him."

"I wish like hell I could love you the way you need to be loved, Payne."

"So do I, but I know Nolan has you all confused right now."

"I wouldn't go that far."

"I'd do anything to make you happy." He ignored me. "I'm ready to start a family with you, regardless of how deeply you're in love with Nolan. We both know you need to get that man out of your system if we're to have any chance of a future. In my eyes, you're the woman I'm meant to have, and nothing is going to stop me from getting you in the end." I used that to my advantage, knowing it would be a long time before he'd be ready to shake me, if ever.

The difficult part was getting on the Rogiers's property. I was pretty sure they had state-of-the-art security. I braced myself, sighed, and got ready to take the long drive up the hill, hoping that I would be able to get into the gated, secluded property without much of a fight.

There was a delivery truck heading that way, and I hoped that it was going to that residence. I watched him coast up to their lot, pause for a second to say something into the intercom, and make his way through the gates. I was directly behind him, determined to get in there, even if I had to get banged up a little bit. I flew past the gate right before it closed. When he parked, I parked, and, as soon as he went up to the front to start doing his deliveries, I went in through another entrance. I was there now, and no one could stop me.

"What the hell are you doing in my house?" Rolanda screeched.

"Hello, Mrs. Rogiers. You may have met me once or twice, but we were never formally introduced," I told her as I extended my hand for her to shake.

"Who are you?" she asked, leaving my hand in midair. "I should have you arrested for coming on my property unannounced."

"I didn't."

"Yes, you did. I authorized the delivery truck that just came in. You entered without permission. I saw you on the security cameras."

"Actually, ma'am, I left something here the other night."

"So, that gives you the right to trespass? What can I do for you, Miss, Miss—?"

"Evette," I interrupted.

"Come to think of it, you do look familiar."

"That's because I'm Nolan's girlfriend."

Rolanda

My family was going bat shit crazy, and I knew there was no way I would rest until I found out what the hell was going on. My sons had lost it on all levels, and they had so many women coming out of the woodwork, I didn't know what to do. I was used to Nolan and Greg's antics, but the lunatic that snuck into my property had to be certifiable, not to mention the wild-eyed chick that was following Dolan around at the party. She was sending off all kinds of red flags.

Even my daughter-in-law had done a one-eighty. We used to talk all the time. But lately, she acted like I was a stranger to her. In the past, when something was going on with Dolan, she would come to me first because she knew I would try to help any way I could. I knew she was stressed out not being able to have a baby, but I couldn't understand why she didn't feel like I would support her in it.

A lot of women had breakdowns when they couldn't get pregnant right away. Sometimes, the stress alone caused them not to be able to conceive. But that didn't mean they gave up. Usually, all it took was for them to calm down, take better care of themselves, and commence to enjoying life, and their bodies accepted a baby in no time. I knew Darica was strong, young, and vibrant, and she would pass that test with flying colors.

When I heard she was pregnant, you couldn't pay me to get off the cloud I was on. I was finally going to be a grandmother!

Now, we were sitting in this cold, unrelenting waiting room, instead of in my house celebrating, and I had no idea what to do. What I did know was, if God gave me a chance, I was going to be the best damn grandmother that child ever laid his eyes on. I just needed Him to turn the saddest day in our lives around. In my heart, I wanted Darica to walk out of that operating room like her old self, but every time I closed my eyes, all I could see was that bloody closet and how hopeless everything looked.

I tried to be strong, but my eyes filled up with tears, and I questioned my own strength. I knew I had Phillip and Mama C for support, but I was the backbone of this family, and everyone looked to me for guidance. Dolan and my mother saw me crying, so they reached over to hug me, followed by April, Chevette, and Nuni.

"Shhhhh," Mama C replied. "It's going to be okay, baby. God is with us, and He'll help us and send us a miracle, so we know He hasn't forgotten about us. God, please take away any flaws and replace them with goodness. Amen."

Suddenly, the double doors opened, and Nolan walked out. He was dressed in scrubs and the white coat he wore whenever he operated on a patient. That was odd because the last time I saw him, he was on his way to the police station, and he wasn't even thinking about work.

"Darica's fine," he said. "She's in recovery now. I know you all want to see her, but no visitors, please. She needs her rest."

Darica

A sharp pain hit me, and I was uncomfortable as all get-out. At first, I didn't know what the hell happened to me, and I struggled to regain my memory. Then I remembered being in a closet, and Nolan, then Dolan, frantically looking for me. It didn't take a scholar to see that they both wanted desperately for me to be okay.

I would later find out that Nolan operated on me and brought me back to life after I died a few times, working feverishly until I was stabilized. When he was done, he wheeled me into a little room off to the side. I was in and out of consciousness, but the one thing that stood out was the love I felt from him and the warmth of his lips when he kissed me and woke me up. I couldn't understand what he was saying, but if I had to guess, I would say he told me how glad he was that I was okay and how much he loved me. Then he caressed my face and exited the room. Something happened in that operating room that I couldn't describe. It's like we connected on a level I never felt with another human being.

Carlena

I made my appearance at the hospital and saw Darica's family waiting to hear her prognosis. I told them how sorry I was about their loved one and continued into my office. The hospital buzz was Darica was wheeled into the operating room, but her life was hanging on a string. I was angry at myself for not going hard enough to kill her, but I was sure I had done enough damage to make them wish I had.

I wished I would have finished Darica off at her wedding, but Captain Save a Ho, aka Nolan, was on me like white on rice and wouldn't let me pull the trigger. Nolan wasn't with his family for some reason, and I was glad of that. Even if he had been, he wasn't scheduled to work today. Dr. Jones was, and his alcoholic ass was a joke if

I ever saw one. I closed my door, put my feet up on my desk, and leaned back in my chair to wait for my answer.

Dolan

I was trying to check in on Darica when Carlena came following behind me. I wanted to take my right foot and shove it right up her ass.

"I'm concerned about Darica," she insisted. "Is there anything I can do?"

I slapped her right cheek so hard, I heard the echo across the room. She instantly grabbed her red face. I was not a fan of violence toward women, but for some reason, I couldn't hold back my anger. I wanted her out of my face and out of the way.

"Don't you ever come in the same room as my wife."

She didn't say anything; she just rubbed her face and walked away.

When I arrived at Darica's bedside, all the monitors she was hooked up to started going off, and Nolan ran in to see what was going on.

"The patient is in distress!" he yelled to no one in particular. Two nurses ran in to check on her.

"What's going on?" I asked.

"Her brain is trying to process the extensive surgery and pain. We had to resuscitate her twice, and I'm pretty sure she's confused and having a stress reaction. I'm going to have to ask you to leave."

"Leave?"

"Just so the patient—"

"The *patient?* You're acting like we're strangers. I'm not leaving my wife!" I yelled.

"Don't you want what's best for her?"

"Are you saying *you're* what's best for her? *I'm* her husband," I reminded Nolan. "She needs *me.*"

"I don't know what you're talking about. I'm just look-ing out for my patient. You want her to get better, don't you?"

"I don't know why you would even question that."

"I know how you feel, bruh, but she can go into shock any minute if we don't give her adequate time to restore. Give her a few hours or come back in the morning."

"Fine," I said. "I'll be back soon."

By this time, our mothers had walked in and tried to fol-low the conversation, but they were too speechless to say anything. They kissed Darica on the cheek and left the hos-pital room. I followed behind them, grateful to finally see my wife resting peacefully.

Darica

After a few hours of sleep, I felt rejuvenated but groggy. I lay there in a near comatose state while listening to the hustle and bustle of hospital staff until a figure came in, and I strained my blurred eyes to see who it was. My eyes adjusted, and I saw Carlena standing over me with a pillow. I thought I was dreaming until I realized she was getting ready to place it on my face and end my life right then and there. I braced myself for the struggle, knowing full well I was too weak for the fight.

"Welcome back, slut. I have to hand it to you. For a weak bitch, you're pretty strong," she laughed uncontrol-lably, leaned down to my left ear, and spoke.

I tried to look around for something to grab, but neither my head nor hands would move. This was crazy because I knew I hadn't cheated death just for her to kill me anyway.

"Unfortunately, I didn't kill your ass, so I came to see if you wanted to take me up on an offer I'm sure you won't refuse. If you keep your mouth shut about me stabbing you, I'll let you live and keep the secret about that bastard child inside you. Do we have a deal?"

I couldn't speak or move, even though my mind was willing. That "bastard child" as she called it, was the only thing I cared about, and I knew I would do anything to keep it safe.

"If you can find some kind of way to let me know you agree, I'll keep the secret about your lover as an added benefit."

I blinked my eyes, and a single tear rolled down my face.

She took that to mean "yes" and added, "Good. It was nice doing business with you."

My monitors started going crazy again, and Carlena knew, without a doubt, I heard her loud and clear. When the nurses came in, she pretended to be concerned. After all, she was the hospital case manager, and her office was right across from my room.

"I think she needs resuscitation, Doctor. You're a pro at that." She smirked when Nolan came in.

Nolan didn't get a chance to answer because he was too busy trying to get me stabilized. Hours later, Nolan came to check on me again. I had had some rest, was feeling much better, and I was able to talk.

"Is everything okay with the baby?"

"The baby is fine," he smiled.

That was music to my ears, and after hearing that, I felt like I could sleep all day. I closed my eyes to savor the moment, but it was short-lived. A detective came to talk to me about my assault.

"Hello, Nolan. We meet again," the detective said.

"Unfortunately," Nolan replied.

"How's she doing?"

"She's doing okay, but now is not a good time to talk. Come back in a few hours."

"Uh-uh. It's important that I talk to her now."

"Give us a minute."

The detective stepped out of the room, and Nolan sat with me for a while. After a few shots and a glass of water, I felt better, and he invited the detective to come back in.

"Keep the questions light, or I'll have to ask you to leave," Nolan warned him.

"You bet," he stated. "Don't worry, Dr. Rogiers. I'm here to help. The sooner we get that crazy person off the street, the better."

"I agree. Let me know if you need me, Darica," Nolan said.

"OK," I nodded.

"So, Mrs. Rogiers—" he started.

"Call me, Darica," I said in a raspy voice as I tried to sit up and winced in pain.

"Thank you, Darica. Do you know anyone who would want to kill you?"

"No."

"Any enemies, run-ins, or arguments?"

"No."

"Does your husband have any baby mamas?"

"No." I didn't bother to tell him my husband couldn't have children.

"Does he have any ex-lovers?"

"None that I know own of," I lied.

"Was there any suspicious person at the party?"

"I didn't notice anyone."

"How about your loved ones, do they have any enemies?"

"If they do, I don't know about it."

"OK. That's all for now. Here's my card and thank you for your time. I'll be in touch."

"Thank you," I said as I gave him a fake smile. Carlena came into the room after he left.

"Good work." She clapped.

"I'm curious," I told her.

"About?"

"Why a woman would want a man who doesn't *want* her," I said that with emphasis and eyed the mark that was on her face.

"It's all about want and need."

"What?"

"Dolan wants you, but he *needs* me."

"And how do you convince him of that?"

"Once you leave him, I'm not going to jump on him right away. I'll let him sow his oats, do his thing for a while."

"That's stupid."

"Actually, it's smart. Jumping in his arms will only make him resent me. Eventually, he'll want me on his own."

I wasn't up for argument, especially about something that sounded crazy as hell. But if she was willing to keep my secrets, I definitely wasn't going to protest. I just knew I had to comply with what she wanted. I loved my husband with all my heart, and I damn sure didn't want him with Carlena or anyone else, but I didn't want to hurt him either.

Dolan walked into my hospital room with so many gifts that he looked more like a street vendor than a proud husband. He had about ten balloons with various quotes that said anywhere from "I love you" to "get well soon," three bouquets of flowers, and two big teddy bears.

To say he was happy to see his wife alive was an understatement. He was ecstatic. I knew I looked pale and sick, and it was obvious he felt sorry for me, but he smiled as if I were my normal, vibrant self.

"Hey, my first love," I mumbled.

"Hey, every breath that I take," he whispered. He didn't say anything to Carlena. She rolled her eyes and walked out.

"Thank you. Everything is beautiful."

"No thanks needed. I'm so happy to see you," he told me as we embraced, and he reached down to kiss me.

"I'm happy to see you too."

"What was Carlena doing here?"

"She came to tell me you slept with her."

"Baby, that was in the past."

"Really, Dolan? She also told me she was your first love." Everybody knew when a woman gave you *that* look and asked you a question, she already knew the answer. He decided to come clean.

"Baby, I messed up."

"I'll say."

"She *was* my first sex partner, but be very clear about this. *You* are my *first* and *only* love."

"So, you fucked her while we were married?"

"I was confused after we got married, and I slept with her a few times, usually after drinking too much, but it meant nothing. I haven't touched her since we've been trying to get the baby. I promise."

"So, what you're really saying is I should only worry about your dick wandering when you're drunk?"

"You don't have to worry at all. I learned my lesson, and I'll never do it again."

I already knew what I was up against. Carlena was no match for me. I couldn't even count on one hand the number of times Dolan stepped out on me with her, so I could hardly judge him after what I did with his brother, no less. I wanted nothing more than to rat Carlena out and watch her ass do some serious prison time, but she had my life in her hands, and she knew secrets I could never tell my husband. Besides, she had a beating with my name on it, and I knew eventually I would give it to her.

"Can you tell me who did this to you?" he asked.

I wanted to say, "Yes, your bitch across the hall." Instead, I gave him the only answer that would save our marriage. "No. I can't remember a thing."

Chapter Three

Nolan

"What the hell is the matter with you, Nolan?" my boss yelled through clenched teeth. "I told you about that procedure in confidence. You weren't supposed to use it until I got it approved."

"I didn't have a choice. It was the only way to save her life."

"That's another problem; it was a conflict of interest because you knew the patient."

"Say what you want, but I wasn't going to sit there and watch Doc Jones butcher her."

"What's going to happen when her family finds out the method was out of protocol?"

"The way it was done is secondary to why it was done, and it saved her life. I would think they'd be happy she's okay. At the end of the day, that's all that really matters. Isn't that what we got in this business for, to save lives?"

"Don't patronize me, Nolan. The medical field is a serious business."

"Everything you touch gets approved, so it's just a matter of paperwork. You can backdate it at that. Don't be mad at me, boss. It went off without a hitch. Your masterpiece worked, and Darica is as good as new."

"Is she the reason for the spring in your step?"

"No."

"You don't have to lie to me, Nolan. It doesn't take a genius to know you're in love with her. I just wish my daughter would see that so she can move on with her life."

"I'm sorry about that."

"It's cool. She'll get over it. She's the only daughter I have left. I wish she'd get her act together. I wish she were more like—"

"Like your other daughter," I finished the sentence for him. "Are you okay, boss?"

"Yes," he said as he swiped away the huge tears in his eyes.

"How did she die, anyway?"

"I still can't talk about it."

"No word on the killer?" I asked.

"Not yet. I doubt they'll ever find out."

"You never know, sir."

"Sorry I snapped at you, Nolan. It was a good thing what you did. I'm glad the procedure worked. Now, we can use it for our other patients."

"No problem, boss. I'm ecstatic about it, and you're famous now."

"I can't take credit for your work."

"You're the innovator. I wouldn't have it any other way." The smile on Dr. Lane's face spoke volumes. He couldn't stay mad at me long. I was like the son he never had. I just wish somebody would get on their job and find out what happened to his daughter. He needed closure.

It was time for my break, and I wanted to grab me a coffee. With the image of Darica's violent assault on my mind, I feared I wouldn't be able to keep any food down. I wasn't going to rest until Darica was safe. Nevertheless, I headed to the cafeteria, but halfway there, I heard someone call out to me.

"Hey, Dr. Feel-good," she said. I cringed when I heard her raspy voice. I hadn't seen her since she propositioned me to have sex against my car, and I didn't plan on seeing her ever again. Shortly after our first little encounter, she was transferred to another hospital in another state. I didn't know the details behind it at the time, but I later found out she was blackmailing doctors. There was even a question about her credentials. Why she was in the same room with me now, I did not know, but I damn sure wanted to find out.

"What's up, Nurse Ratchet?" I called her by her newly made-up nickname.

"Actually, my name is Lala. I see you're still bitter about our last little talk, but no love lost. You still make my heart rate rise."

"Too bad the feelings aren't mutual," I said as I pushed past her.

"Don't be like that, baby. We can make it work."

"Nice try, Ratchet, but you know the rules against sexually harassing coworkers."

"What's the charge for making love to patients?"

"What?"

"You're walking around here playing the hero who saved your patient, but I think you did it because you're sprung."

Before I could protest, she showed me a video on her phone. On it was a clip of me kissing Darica on the lips in the recovery room. *Shit,* I said in my mind. I tried to grab her phone, but she was too quick.

"Not so fast, lover. Don't we have some unfinished business?"

"What do you want?"

"You know my fantasy. I just want to spend a little quality time with you on the Ferrari. Meet me in the parking lot."

"Oh, hell no," I told her. I might have been born on a Wednesday, but I wasn't born yesterday. If she thought

I was fucking her on these hospital grounds after she just threatened to turn me in for sexual harassment, she was loonier than I thought. "Why don't I meet you somewhere exotic? I'll call you with the details."

"I told you I have a car fetish."

"You'll get your wish."

"Cool. Here's my phone. Put your number in," she said. I did as I was instructed and pushed *send*. My own phone immediately started ringing. I saw her number pop up and nodded.

"Got it. I'll be in touch."

"Don't make me wait long," she told me.

"I wouldn't dream of it," I said.

The thought of going to my empty house was depressing. It wasn't for lack of anything to do. I had a pretty active social life if I cared to resume it, not to mention the many women who were still ringing my phone. But I learned a long time ago not to settle for hamburger when steak was on the menu. If anyone had told me last year that I was going to fall in love with someone, and that same woman was going to have me crazy for her the way Darica had me now, I would have told them they needed to see a psychiatrist. But it was no secret that I would rather spend my spare time up at the hospital playing Monopoly with her than anything else. I had built a mansion fit for a boss, and she was the only queen I wanted in it.

I was almost to the parking lot, but I had to have one last glimpse of her. At least, that's what my mind told me as I made my way to her room. The hospital was fairly empty, but I told her nurse to take a long break, just in case. Darica looked so peaceful lying in her hospital bed that it almost felt like a crime to disturb her. That's when

I saw her put her hand under the sheet and move it up and down on her pelvis. Damn. I was watching Darica pleasure herself, and it was better than anything on TV. I listened to her soft moans, and it brought my dick to attention right away. "Shit," I whispered so loud, it made her flinch. If she heard me, she didn't show it. She kept doing what she was doing, and it was so sexy; my eyes were stuck to her like glue, even as I closed the door and the curtain and thanked the good Lord that she didn't have a roommate. By now, she was writhing in pleasure as her hand did the work to bring her release. She didn't even notice that the room had become darker from the door being closed. It wasn't uncommon for patients to turn to self-gratification when they were in pain. Sometimes, it worked better than medication.

"Let me help you with that," I told her as I positioned my mouth inches above her.

"Damn, Nolan. You scared the shit out of me," she hissed. I ignored her and connected my tongue to her clit. "Stop," she hesitantly replied.

"Don't be shy," I commanded. "Just let me work my magic." She tried to push me away, but she was no match for my persevering tongue and too weak to protest.

"Please don't make me do this."

"You need it."

"Uuuuum, Nolan. That feels good."

"Come for me," I urged.

"Stop."

"Is that what you want?"

"No. Don't stop," she ordered.

"Never," I promised and kept diving into her creamy flesh. She was writhing and moaning so loud that I had to reach up and cover her mouth.

"Nolan. Oh my God, Nolan. Yessssss. I'm about to come."

"Come on," I told her once, and that was enough. She was already filling my mouth with her juices. After she relieved herself, she fell asleep almost instantly. "Good night," I told her as I kissed her on the forehead and went into the bathroom to clean up before heading home. Now, we both were happy.

I was feeling good as hell, had made it halfway to my car when the alarm went off, and I looked up to make sure no one had broken in. I saw a figure standing next to it and thought it was Nurse Ratchet jumping the gun. I was definitely going to meet up with her because I needed to put that mess behind me. Nothing was going to taint what Darica and I just shared. Upon careful speculation, though, I saw it was Evette. She had on a coat, and I was pretty sure little else under it.

"What do you want?" I spat.

"You."

"I'm not feeling you like that." She ignored me, opened the coat, and I didn't feel a thing for the panty-bra set that, months ago, had set me ablaze.

"We can rekindle some of that old passion. It'll be just like old times."

"No, thank you. I have somewhere to be."

"Where do you live anyway? I went by your house a few times, and it was empty."

"I moved."

"If you don't feel comfortable doing it out here, give me the address, and I'll meet you at the new house."

"I don't want you."

"So, you're not going to give it to me?"

"So you can stalk me like you're doing now?"

"Don't be like that, baby."

"Go play in traffic, Evette. I've moved on. You need to do the same."

"I can't be without you, baby. We were supposed to get married."

"Girl, bye."

"If this is about Darica, she's married already."

I pushed her out of the way, jumped in my car, and sped off.

Evette

My phone was ringing off the hook. I had just gotten rid of company, and I was determined to get some sleep.

"Who the hell is this, and what do you want this early?"

"It's Carlena."

Carlena and I went way back. We were friends since we met at the hospital, got close, and learned through conversation that we were both in love with the Rogiers brothers. She had a huge crush on Nolan, and I was, of course, in love with Dolan. We would do anything to get the men in our lives, including wipe Darica off the face of the earth.

"Where the hell are you? I've been trying to reach you forever."

"I had business to attend to."

"Like what?"

"Like killing Darica."

"When I left from over there, they were still looking for her. Is the bitch dead?"

"Unfortunately, not."

"What did you try to kill her for if you weren't going to succeed?"

"I did more than you did. You were just sitting around."

"Nobody told you to take the job when you obviously couldn't handle it. I had it in the bag."

"Yeah, right. Bitch, you're getting soft."

"If I would've tried to kill her ass, she'd be gone by now. Your ass is an amateur. So, what happened anyway?"

"I stabbed her up, but, apparently, I didn't hit the right spot."

"I know she's a headache, but you can't go all crazy. You have to stay cool."

"Oh yeah? Well, let's see how much you keep your cool when you hear what I have to say."

"What?"

"Nolan saved her life."

"Say *what?*"

"Yeah, you heard me right. He used some hotti totti procedure that's only been tested overseas or something. If it weren't for him, she would've died. She's probably falling into his arms as we speak."

"That's some fairy-tale bullshit. Who does that?"

"Nolan."

"She doesn't want him. She's in love with her husband."

"You mean the husband who's gonna break up with her when I tell him she fucked around with his brother?"

"Before or after they haul your ass to jail?"

"I got her to promise she wouldn't tell, in exchange for keeping her secret."

"Bitch, you're lying."

"If I'm lying, I'm dying, and I'm very much alive. I worked out a little deal with her. I told her if she talks, I'll go straight to Dolan and tell him what she did."

"But you're going to do that anyway."

"So what? She doesn't have to know that."

"You're pitiful. That's all good for you because you'll have your man. What about me?"

"I got a couple of suggestions for you if you're interested."

"Yeah. Maybe we can come up with something that will help me because Nolan is all the way gone."

"Okay. I'll be at your house at about noon."

"Sounds good. I'll see you then."

I was too through with Nolan. After all I had done for his ungrateful ass, he still had the nerve and audacity to shun me like I was a bitch off the street. Right before he started screwing around with his sister-in-law, I felt like we were getting somewhere. Even though I was lying through my teeth when I said I was pregnant, he didn't believe a word I said. I wasn't getting any younger, and I wanted to get my family started before it was too late. I wished Carlena had killed Darica's ass because she was nothing but dead weight. Women like her had it all—a good husband, a home, a family, and a boatload of friends, but they usually end up throwing it all away. As mad as I was about her letting Nolan walk in and knock the bottom out her world, I couldn't even blame her because the man was the shit, and I wanted him more than my next breath.

I ate a bowl of cereal, picked out my outfit for the day, and headed into the bathroom to shower when I heard what sounded like broken glass. I noticed it came from my kitchen, so I replaced the towel I had wrapped around me with a bathrobe and went to investigate. As soon as I rounded the corner . . . I saw her. The prostitute I thought I killed was standing there with gauze wrapped around her midsection like a mummy, and she looked weak. I had stabbed her for having sex with Nolan. In my mind, she was a threat, as was any woman who slept with Nolan, but as usual, once I found out that he didn't want her, it was too late. I had already wounded her. I knew I should have buried her ass after, but I didn't. Now she had found me and was holding a gun in her hand, so I decided to try to reason with her.

I took one look at her and knew she wasn't having it. I didn't have a chance in hell of getting out unless I played nice, so I apologized and tried to walk toward her. She put a bullet through my shoulder without a second thought. It grazed me but hurt like hell. I prayed someone would hear the gunshot, then remembered *I* didn't even hear the gun go off. She had a silencer on her weapon. I wanted to run, but the pain was too unbearable. I wanted to beg for my life, but she didn't seem to have any mercy. I fell to the ground bleeding, wondering if this was it for me.

Darica

I woke up to the hustle and bustle of hospital activity and noticed, once again, that I hadn't been greeted or washed up. If I could've gotten my ass up out of that bed and done it myself, it would definitely be a wrap. The board in front of my bed was empty because no nurse had written her name or even the date, for that matter, for the second time in as many days. I figured it had to be the same nurse I had last time I woke up like this because when she finally did get around to coming in, she didn't greet me or acknowledge me, except to roll her eyes at me like I slept with her ass last night. She must've been having a bad day because she came in with an attitude the size of Texas, and I wasn't surprised at all when she didn't ask me if I needed anything or try to adjust me in the bed.

"Can I get some water?" I asked.

"Yeah," she said abruptly, then walked back out. *What is with this bitch of a nurse from hell?* I wondered. She came back with the water and almost spilled it on me by pounding the pitcher on my bed table. It wasn't cold and tasted horrible. Then she pulled out her cell phone and started texting.

"Um . . . Can you give me some more water, preferably some with ice that doesn't taste like shit is in it?"

"Give me a sec," she spat like I was invading her quiet time or her break or something she was enjoying before I rudely interrupted.

"Do you have a problem with me?"

"No, I don't know you're a—I mean, you, from a can of paint. Why would you say that?"

"You seem to have an attitude. I mean, I know everybody has bad days, but this is the second time you've been my nurse, and you treat me like crap. I don't know your name because you didn't write it on the board, and you're downright disrespectful. I paid my money, just like everybody else in this hospital."

There was an unusually long silence, where one would think she would have some concern for what I was saying, but she just looked at me with disdain, grabbed the pitcher of hot water, and stormed out. I usually didn't make a big deal or push to get people in trouble, but I had to make a complaint because this was just too much. I pushed the call button and waited for someone at the nurse's station to answer.

"Yes," someone answered.

"I want a new nurse. This one has an attitude problem."

"Don't they all, honey?" she asked, then added, "but I'll see what I can do."

Not only did I *not* get a new nurse, but they must have told my current one what I said because she came in my room with lukewarm water, gave me a rough sponge bath, and barely gave me a clean gown to put on. "Oh, it's cool, bitch. I got something for you," I mumbled.

After dealing with her shenanigans, I definitely needed something to cheer me up. I thought about Dolan and me in happier times, particularly when we were trying to conceive.

***

The first time Dolan and I called ourselves "making a baby," we were so ecstatic; we carefully planned it, right down to the very day of conception. I got off the pill, and Dolan stopped using condoms. We saw a doctor, and both of us got on a special diet so we would be off to a healthy start in becoming parents. We wanted a fall baby, so, on New Year's Eve at approximately six o'clock in the evening, we began our mating ritual. Even then, my husband was full of surprises, insisting we eat our dinner in the den.

I was bringing in the food on little platters when I noticed Dolan had removed the only table we had in there and replaced it with a plastic tablecloth on the floor. He had strategically placed a blue sheet, dry washcloths, and a bowl of warm, soapy water next to that. When he came in, he took the food from me and put it on the sheet and carefully laid me on the tablecloth.

"I told you I was making you dinner," he said with a wink. Right then and there, I understood what he meant. He wasted no time spooning the teriyaki chicken and rice on my stomach and breasts and ate it off me until he was full. Then he lay on the sheet, and I did the same thing to him. By the time we washed ourselves with the warm, soapy cloths, we were so turned on that we barely made it to our bed. Without the confines of birth control, we felt totally free to do whatever we wanted sexually, and that's exactly what we did. I came so many times, I lost count, and so did Dolan. I was almost certain we were pregnant, but we continued the ritual over and over, determined to do so until I showed signs of pregnancy or a missed a period. But every month . . . nothing happened.

Eventually, we only made love when I was ovulating, when we felt lucky, and finally, went back to only doing it when we were in the mood. I didn't tell my husband, but I hated any time someone made a reference to having a baby, hated seeing babies in the grocery store, hated hearing them cry, and dreaded when my mother-in-law mentioned she didn't have any grandkids. I was about ready to throw my hands up and say to hell with everything. Depression was an understatement. I was determined to experience motherhood at any cost. It was stealing my joy. I guess my little situation caused me to do things I never thought I would do, and I went overboard.

My little trip down memory lane faded when I heard voices coming down the hallway.

The ladies were literally a sight for sore eyes. Rolanda was leading the pack. She had on a cream Donna Karen dress with Choo heels, her hair in a tight bun, and her face was beat to the gods. April was right behind her. My bestie was rocking a yellow jumpsuit that accentuated her voluptuous curves and long Brazilian locks that cascaded her beautiful, natural face. Chevette wasn't too far behind them. I almost didn't recognize her in her navy Gucci dress paired with matching heels, earrings, sunglasses, and bag. Her powder-blue nails and feet set it off wonderfully. Gone was the lack of confidence Greg had instilled in her.

"Hey, beautiful," Rolanda said as they all took turns bending down to kiss me. She must've been lying to me because I felt anything but. Mama C walked in a few seconds later and kissed me on the cheek.

"How are you feeling?" she asked.

"I've definitely had better days."

"Damn, chica. I've never been so scared in my life," April said.

"I'm glad you're okay," Chevette added.

"Me too," I said.

"I hope they catch your attacker," April said.

"Me too. I gave them tons of info, so that's a start," I lied.

"Too bad you didn't recognize the bastard who did this. Please believe, they got an ass whooping coming with my name on it," April stated. I hated lying to them, but I planned to get first dibs on Carlena, even if I had to wait until I gave birth to do it.

"Thanks, chica. I'm just glad I survived it."

"Thanks to God," Rolanda added.

"Nolan had a hand in it too," Chevette said.

"Wait. What?" I sat up to say.

"Not only did he find you in the house and stabilized you, he damn near kicked your doctor out of the operating room and performed the surgery himself."

"Where'd you hear that at?" April asked.

"I have a friend who works at the hospital," Chevette said.

Nuni walked in looking like new money. He was smiling so hard, I thought his lips were stuck to his teeth.

"Girlfriend, I told these nonbelievers you were a fighter, and nothing was going to happen to you."

"Apparently, Nolan made sure of that," April repeated.

"I already knew that!" Nuni screeched. "Everybody in this hospital is talking about it. They say the procedure has only been done three times and only once in America. You're lucky as hell to know him."

"I'm proud of my Nolan," Rolanda smiled.

"That's *my* grandson," said Mama C.

I couldn't lie. The information floored me, and even more so when I thought about what Nolan said to me in the closet and did with his tongue. He wanted me bad, and I felt grateful—and sorry—at the same time. I had escaped death once by Carlena's hand, but there was no telling what *his* girlfriend had in store for me. The best thing for me to do was be by myself, and I wasn't sure if I could do it while I was pregnant. I could barely look Rolanda in the eye, knowing I had slept with both her sons, and I was almost certain Mama C saw right through me.

Just then, my anesthesiologist Gregg (with two *g*'s) peeked in the door.

"Come in," I grinned. He barely walked in the room when his whole face lit up. I knew he wasn't excited over my raggedy ass, but when I saw Chevette blush, I knew he was coming for her.

"This is the friend I was telling y'all about," she gushed.

"Damn," April and Nuni said at the same time.

"How's my favorite patient?" he asked.

"I'm fine," I answered.

"You are quite the miracle."

"Yes. But I can't take all the credit. I had a good doctor, and you are absolutely incredible. Thanks a million."

"No problem at all. Are we still watching the game?" he asked Chevette. He hadn't taken his eyes off her since he came in.

"Of course, we are. I have to make sure I collect when your sorry team loses."

"See, that's where you're wrong. Your team don't have a chance."

"Just make sure you bring cash."

"OK. Meet me at Massey's and don't be late this time."

"Cool," she said as she watched him walk away and pulled out her cell phone to pretend she was checking the time.

"Oh no, bitch. Don't even try it," Nuni said. Truth be told, I was going to speak up if he hadn't.

"What? Him? That's my friend. We've been knowing each other since we were kids."

"You ain't no kid now," April reminded her. "He's tall, dark, and handsome with pretty teeth and waves for days. I bet he didn't have all that in grade school."

"It's no big deal, April."

"Sheeitttttt!" Nuni screamed. "Oops, sorry, Mama C."

"I understand," Mama C sang.

"When were you going to tell us, Miss Thing?" Nuni asked, not letting her get out of it for one second.

"At the next girlz nite," Chevette smiled. "You won't be here anyway."

"The hell if I'm not. I'm not going anywhere until my girlfriend is fully recovered."

"Looks like the cat's out of the bag," I grinned.

"It's not that serious. Damn," Chevette said.

"Looks like you're moving on with your life," Rolanda added.

"I just don't want to sit around and mope about my husband," Chevette said as she folded her arms. "It's tough."

"I ain't even mad!" April shouted.

Nolan walked in and waved. Everybody clapped.

"There's my grandson," said Mama C. "Everybody's talking about you."

"Hopefully, it's something good," he smiled.

"It's excellent. I'm so proud of you, son," Rolanda exclaimed.

"It was nothing, Ma," he blushed.

"It was *everything*," I said as I smiled at him, and he grinned like a Cheshire cat.

"I hate to be the bearer of bad news, but I came to tell you guys to keep it down. Some of the patients are complaining about the noise."

"We're so sorry," Rolanda said.

"Actually, we were just leaving," April added.

"My girl needs her beauty sleep," said Nuni.

"I'll see you tomorrow, love," Chevette added.

"I better. You know I'm anxious to hear about that date—uh, I mean . . . game."

"Most definitely. Get some rest."

"I'll be back tomorrow. I love you, chica," April said.

"Get well soon, daughter," Rolanda told me.

"I'm praying for a speedy recovery," Mama C said as she kissed my forehead.

As each one reached over to hug me, I felt nothing but warm, loving arms surround me, and I realized they loved me with all their heart. I couldn't help but think that one day, I'd have to pull them aside, one by one, and tell them the truth. I wondered how many would abandon me, and which ones would stand beside me then. But that would not be my fight today.

"Can you ladies do me one more favor?"

"Sure," they said in unison.

"My nurse is a bitch. Can you handle her for me?"

"My pleasure," April said.

"No, I got this one," Nuni said. Nolan watched them all walk out, then sat on the edge of my bed.

"How are you feeling?" he asked.

"I'm still in a lot of pain."

"Anything I can do to help?" he asked.

"You did plenty," I blushed. I could still feel his tongue on me.

"I'll have the nurse, the nice one, bring you something."

"That will be great. I want to thank you formally."

"No thanks needed, beautiful. I'm just glad you and our baby are okay."

"I was going to ask about that."

"The baby is fine. Anything else you need, Mommy?"

I wanted to say something, but he seemed so happy. I couldn't tell him that I planned to terminate the pregnancy. I decided to save that for another day.

"No, thank you. I have everything I need."

"So do I," he smiled.

Chapter Four

Dolan

Before I could get to the car, I broke out my flask and took a deep swig. The first thing I thought about was beating Carlena's ass, and that wasn't even me, so I had to have something to hold me down. I hit the freeway going about eighty, then slowed down to fifty-five. The last thing I needed was to get pulled over and slapped with a DUI. I wanted to get home to the unfinished bottle I had in the cabinet.

As soon as I put my key in the door, my phone started ringing. I didn't care who it was; one thing was sure, they were going to be second to this whiskey right now. Jack Daniel was about to change my life. I threw the phone on the couch, ran to the kitchen, grabbed the bottle, and took it to the head. The next thing I knew, I was passed out at the table, dreamt I was lying in bed with Darica, and a hooded man came into our room.

"Take whatever you want, man," I told him. "Just don't hurt us."

"I plan to," the stranger blurted while he pulled the covers back, exposed my wife who only had on a T-shirt and thong, scooped her in his arms, and ran for the door.

"I wasn't talking about my damn wife!" I yelled.

He laughed and said, "She's mine now." Funny thing was he had piercing green eyes and an evil, almost creaturelike face. I tried to pry her out of his hands, but

he was ten times stronger than I was. I beat his arms
with my fists, but my hits didn't even make him flinch.

"Darica!" I yelled as he walked out of the house with
her.

I woke up in a cold sweat, thanking my lucky stars it
was a nightmare, but it left a nasty taste in my mouth.
The shit was scary, and I didn't know what the hell it
meant. But one thing was for sure. I wasn't about to let
Carlena's bitch ass run my life. I knew something was
going on when I saw her hovering over Darica in the
hospital. If that bitch touched a hair on her head, she was
going to be sorry she ever met me, and I meant that with
everything within me.

I wasn't about to sit there and defend myself to Darica.
Once my wife made up her mind about something, she
was pretty stubborn, and she stuck to her guns. I decided
to let her cool down, but in the meantime, I was definitely
going to talk to Carlena's ass. Why would she wait all
this time to say something? I know we talked a lot of
mess over the years, but we still found ourselves in bed
with each other, despite it. I wasn't proud of the fact I
stepped out on my wife with her, but it was convenient at
the time. I thought we had an understanding that it was
just sex between two horny adults who knew what they
were getting into and could handle the aftermath. I was
obviously the only one who didn't have trouble letting go.

When I pulled up to her house, I saw her car in the
driveway, which assured me someone was home. I assaulted her door, and anyone within earshot knew that I
was trying to get in that bitch.

"Coming!" I heard her yell. She came to the door in a
see-through nighty that left nothing to the imagination.
I could see her huge, black, stiff nipples through the
gauzy material.

"Dolan," she said, feigning surprise. "What can I do for you?" She licked her lips hungrily and eyed my zipper. The last two times I came to her door, it started off just like this, progressed to her on her knees and my dick in her mouth, and ended with her on all fours screaming my name as I buried every inch of my manhood deep inside her walls. She closed her eyes for a fleeting moment, and I knew she was thinking about it, and no doubt, hoping for a repeat session.

"I came here to tell you that you and I are over, and there will never be anymore 'us.' Do you understand?"

"Yes, Dolan. I am so sorry. I had a moment of weakness. Carlos and I—"

"Carlos?" I blurted.

"Carlos and I broke up, and I got to thinking about how good you were to me. I foolishly thought I wanted to get back with you, but I love him."

"Why did you cause confusion in my marriage?"

"Like I said, it was a mistake."

"How would you like it if I showed up and messed things up between you and old boy?"

"I would be devastated. Like I said, it won't happen again. I promise."

I was taken aback, but, nevertheless, her story seemed reasonable.

"OK. It's cool. I'm going to try to patch things up with my wife."

"I hope everything works out with the two-timing slut."

"What did you say?"

"I said good luck," she said.

"Don't be a smart-ass. For the past three weeks, you showed up at my job, my bank, and even at the car wash trying to get me to slip up and fuck you. You showed up at our house with two kids dressed in Girl Scout outfits pretending you were helping them sell cookies. The final straw was when I had my head down picking flavors, you got all in my face begging me to be with you."

"I said I was sorry."

"It was a good thing the girls had already started walking to the next house. I don't know what I would've done if Nolan and, God forbid, Darica would've opened the front door. As far as I know, my wife had never seen you and didn't know you from the next thot until you showed up in that clinic, but I'm pretty sure my brother would've wasted no time bringing her up to speed."

"Thot?"

"That's all you heard, huh?"

"You don't have to call me out my name. I already apologized. What else do you want me to do?"

"Nothing. I'm just glad you moved on. Whoever Carlos is, I want to thank him for taking you off my hands. You're a fucking handful."

"You have trust issues."

"If you were a halfway decent human being, I would be able to trust you. Looking back on it all, I don't know why I ever did. You knew Miko was crazy about me when we were younger, yet you pretended to be her friend, and for some reason, I have a feeling you had something to do with her going off the deep end."

"You weren't complaining then."

"Because I couldn't see past what I wanted. I let you use me because of my own selfish needs. But you're blatantly jealous of the women in my life, and the only thing I was to you was your pawn. I thought I was the one in control, but I didn't know nothing about sex or love, and I fell for you hard. I'm so glad I woke up."

She just looked at me through the slits of her eyes, unable to respond to my rant. I shook my head, left her standing there, and walked away.

***

As soon as I got home, I went to the clinic website to check our profile, hoping Darica didn't shut down the account before I got a chance to check it to see if there was someone we could speak to about our marriage. Maybe they had a professional that could shed light on the ins and outs of artificial insemination and, if all else failed, a new donor that would be better suited, in case she went off and terminated the current pregnancy and decided to have a baby later. I also wanted to make sure Carlena was taken off our case. I simply did not and could not trust her.

As I made my way through the website, a caption caught my attention. It said *Number of Successful Treatments*. Beside it was a big fat *zero*. I called the 800 number to ask a question I was afraid to get the answer to.

"Clinic," the receptionist answered.

"How often is the website updated?" I cut right to the chase and asked.

"Daily," she replied.

"So, if the treatment were successful a few weeks ago, it would automatically update the next day?"

"Absolutely," she said.

"Are you sure?" I asked.

"I'm positive," she said.

"There must be something wrong with my account because my wife got pregnant, and the website is saying that none of the treatments were successful. Is there any explanation for that?"

"No, sir. If the treatments were successful, it would say so. Maybe you guys lucked up and got pregnant on your own. That's definitely a possibility."

I didn't bother telling her the details. I simply said, "Thank you," and hung up. If I hadn't heard the voicemail from the clinic in Nebraska on Darica's birthday myself,

I would probably think my wife took a home pregnancy test that gave her the wrong results. She wasn't even happy enough to tell me.

After scrolling the block for a young woman who sounded like Darica and paying her twenty dollars, I gave her the phone number to call the clinic in Nebraska to get further confirmation to my question.

Darica was definitely pregnant.

I called to set an appointment with a local specialist to have him check my sperm count and got one for the same day. I was on pins and needles as I waited in the reception area. I didn't know what to think, but I kept an open mind.

"Are you taking any medications, Mr. Rogiers?" the doctor asked.

"Yes, I'm taking these," I said as I held up the bottle of pills I had taken for months.

"I thought you said you were trying to get your wife pregnant," he said with a puzzled expression.

"Yes. We've been trying for months."

"Well, this prescription is a medication that will keep you from getting a woman pregnant."

"That's got to be a mistake. The doctor that gave me these was adamant that I take them, so I'd have a better chance of increasing my sperm count."

"Either he's an amateur, a prankster, or plain crazy because these pills will *never* help you get anyone pregnant. They do the opposite."

"So, you're telling me that I could have gotten my wife pregnant had I not been taking these pills?"

"It's a strong possibility, Mr. Rogiers. How 'bout I run all the necessary tests and let you know?"

"That would be great," I said. My heart was racing a mile a minute, and I was seething with anger. I'd been trying to get Darica pregnant forever—only to find out this shit.

I wanted to know who the hell was responsible, and once I did, I planned to get revenge in a big way. After the good doctor ran the tests, he confirmed that I had a very healthy sperm count, and I made a beeline to the hospital to confront the doctor who gave me the prescription. Lo and behold, I found out he was fired weeks ago, and there were several malpractice suits against him. It was a good thing he was gone because if I ever saw that fucker again, he would be looking at the end of my right hook.

There were times when I stopped taking that medicine for days, even weeks, because it didn't seem to be doing much of anything. I wasn't sure how effective it was if I wasn't taking it consistently, but if the pills were as potent as my new doctor said, there was little hope for me at all. The fact that I knew there was even a slight chance I could be the father of my wife's baby should have made me feel better, but it didn't because all the signs pointed to the fact she had an affair.

Evette

By the time noon rolled around, I had slipped in and out of consciousness. The hooker, whose name I found out was Essence, had bandaged up my shoulder and took care of the wound. I figured she planned to keep me around for a while, or I'd be dead. I prayed she wasn't going to torture me because I wasn't built for that.

"Whatever you're going to do, do it quickly."

"Shut up, bitch," she told me. "You don't get to call any shots."

"What do you want?"

"I want to shoot you in your mouth," she threatened as she waved the gun in the air. "Shut up before I do it."

I did as I was told and turned to watch the television to keep my mind off the pain. Suddenly, there was a knock on the door, and I knew it was Carlena.

"Go open the door. Don't try anything funny, or I'll shoot you in the back of your head."

I went to the door and opened it, so my left shoulder didn't show. "Hey, girl. I'll have to meet up with you some other time," I told her.

"What do you mean some other time? I'm here now. Why are you sweating like that? I hope you're not contagious."

"I'm not feeling well. Can I call you tomorrow or something?"

"Don't play, Evette. Time is of the essence, so let's get this over with. I need to get back to preparing for my man."

I was sweating and trembling from the pain. I know I must've looked like I was going to pass out, but I was out of excuses. The hooker knew it too because she pressed the gun more firmly in the back of my head as she stood behind me. Seconds went by, and we both realized Carlena wasn't going to leave.

"Come on in, Carlena," she said. Carlena was puzzled at hearing the strange voice behind me, but she came in anyway.

"Looks like I got two for the price of one," the hooker said. We both looked at her like she was crazy as she motioned for us to sit on the couch.

Dolan

Since the business venture I had negotiated with my dad to open a restaurant was placed on hold, I interrupted my leave of absence to go back to work. My boss was drowning in paper, and he needed all the help he could get. The day was pretty slow, which was fine for me because I wasn't feeling like dealing with too many people anyway.

I walked into the waiting area, and the first thing that caught my eye was Tonette's breasts. They were straining against the fabric of her brown catsuit, which was a wonder in itself. Everywhere you turned, a man was ogling her. She was sitting there with her right leg crossed over her left, filing her perfectly manicured beige nails like she was in a beauty shop. Her eyes got big as saucers when she saw me. I smiled and waved for her to follow me to my cubicle.

"Hey, handsome," she said.

"Hello, Tonette. What brings you here today?"

"I wanted to update my file."

"Oh? Did you get a new car?"

"No."

"Need to add a new driver?"

"Uh-uh."

"Did you get into an accident?"

"Hell, no."

"Why don't you fill me in, then?"

"I came to give you my new number." I was speechless for about ten seconds, looking at her like she was crazy the whole time.

"You could've called the 800 number to do that."

"I was in the area, and I wanted to see you."

"Why?"

"Let's stop playing these games, Dolan."

"I told you I was married."

"You're not happy."

"Yes, I am," I said, almost choking on my own words. She eyed me sympathetically and grabbed my hands.

"You look like you could use a friend." I gripped her hands and squeezed them tightly.

"You're right," I told her.

"Why don't we meet up after you get off?" she said. "I can't cook, but I make a mean martini."

"I can bring pizza," I added.

"It's a deal," she smiled.

When I got off work, I stopped at home to take a quick shower and throw on something more comfortable. I put on some True Religion jeans, a short sleeve, button-down shirt, and some Jordans. I had just grabbed my keys when my phone started ringing. The caller ID said Lake Hospital. I only answered because I wanted to make sure Darica was okay. I felt a little guilty about hanging out with another woman while she was stuck in bed. Then I recovered when I thought about the fact *she* was the very reason I was in this predicament. Yes, I had cheated, but once I saw the light, I became fully committed to my marriage and didn't deserve to be mistreated. I only accepted Tonette's invitation to get my mind off my problems.

"Hello."

"Hi, Dolan. I just wanted to check in with you," Darica sang.

"I'm fine. What's up?"

"I just wanted to let you know how difficult this is for me."

"I feel the same way, Darica, but we can't take it back. We either accept it and stay together or go on with our lives."

"I think we should take it slow."

"We'll make it work," I said.

"I don't think we should get back together yet. We both made some serious mistakes, and I'm not sure this is going to work."

"Fine, then. Take all the time you need."

"Thank you."

"You're welcome. Get well soon, love."

"I will."

My heart broke in a million pieces at hearing Darica say she wanted to put a hold on our marriage. I wanted to be her husband until I took my last breath, but the fact that she was trying to back out of the relationship showed me my options were limited, especially if she cheated, and most definitely if she were pregnant by another man.

Chapter Five

Nolan

Massey's was so crowded that I barely had room to breathe. If Greg hadn't called me to come, I would've taken my happy ass out and marched right back to the hospital to sit with Darica. She was tearful, even after I changed her medication three times. I knew something was terribly wrong . . . aside from the fact she had almost died from a brutal stabbing. I knew she suffered from post-traumatic stress disorder (PTSD), and I had her set up for therapy within the next couple of days. I couldn't help but wonder if Evette stabbed her. She was getting more desperate by the minute, and I knew that cutting her off was the best thing I ever did.

Dolan was on some crazy shit too. I called him a few times, and he was cold to me—if he even bothered to answer my calls at all. I knew he was still salty about all the attention I was showing Darica, but I'd known him long enough to know it went deeper than that. This whole thing started off great with me reconciling with my brother, but it all went left in a matter of months. That's how it always ended. But somehow, I felt we would never get it right. Sooner or later, we were going to have to tell Dolan what we did, so we could all move on with our lives. A child was now a part of this equation and needed all the support it could get. Suddenly, I was sad about how it all went down. I regretted the day I fell for Darica, and I was bitter about Dolan marrying her.

I made my way over to the bar, but there was nowhere to sit. I stood behind an old man, who looked like he was about to fall off the bar stool, and looked around for Greg, but he was nowhere to be found. That's when I saw the breaking news on one of the television monitors. One caption said: *One woman dead and one found . . .* with pictures of my former coworker, Sheila, and Mina. Another caption said the prostitute, Essence, was still missing, and they hadn't found her yet. The hospital serial killer was at large way before I even started at the hospital, so I knew they had their work cut out for them. I was happy to know that they had found Mina in a quiet suburb a few miles away. I guess after our so-called breakup, she just wanted to get away.

This calls for a celebration, I thought as I ordered my scotch and soda without any sign of Greg. I drank three rounds and was starting to get wobbly when he finally decided to walk in.

"You look like shit," I told him.

"Thanks a lot, man. I feel like it too."

"What's going on with you?"

"It's Chevette. She left me, man."

"You said that before, and you were wrong."

"I think this is it, this time. First, she moved out, and now, I hear she's dating some bozo from the hospital."

"Listen, that woman loves you. She's just playing a game."

"Yeah? Well, she's winning."

"Don't say that, man. You guys are going to make it. You just need to stop fucking around, that's all."

"You're hardly an advisor, but you make sense. I'm done with that life. I haven't touched Rella or any other woman, for that matter."

"But are you really ready?"

"What do you mean by that?"

"If Chevette were to come back right now, can you honestly say you won't touch another woman?"

"I'm past ready. This really scared me, man. I love her more than anything, and I want to make our marriage work."

"You better fight for her then. I know if it were my marriage, I would."

"You?"

"Yes, me. Man. I'm ready to settle down right now."

"That's what's up, man. Give me the daps."

I dapped my brother up and ordered his usual.

"Thanks, man," he said after a few sips. "So, who's the lucky woman? Hopefully, it's not Darica like Dolan thinks."

"Is that what he thinks?"

"Yeah, to be honest with you, I think it too. There are a million women in the world. Why her?"

"That's a very long and complicated story," I said. I wanted to confide in someone. I really did. But two things stopped me. One, this was our brother I was talking to, and, two, Rella came in the bar like a bat out of hell. She had her mother with her and their baby.

"What the hell is wrong with you, Rella?" Greg asked. "Why you got my daughter up in a bar, and what the hell is your mother doing in here?"

"What the hell you mean, what am I doing in here? What the hell are *you* doing in here?" her mother asked. "You have not answered any of my daughter's calls."

"Just because she said it's my child doesn't mean it is. Now, it's time for her to prove it. As much as I love this little girl, I'm not trying to take care of a seed that's not mine."

"You don't take care of her anyway," Rella retorted.

"I take care of you, though. What have *you* been doing with the money?"

Rella was silent as she started twirling her freshly manicured fingers in her weave. "OK. I'm gonna let you have that one 'cause that's where it ends. I'm trying to get my wife back. I don't have time for your games, and I don't want to talk to you if it doesn't have anything to do with this sweet thing," Greg said as he tickled the baby's tummy, causing her to laugh. "So, don't call me for no bs," he said directly to Rella.

"I can't believe you're treating me like this after all we've been to each other."

"I can't believe I ever messed with your trifling butt," he said, using the clean version because of the kid. "Get the baby out of here."

Rella's mother opened her mouth to say something, but Rella reached out her hand to silence her, did as she was told, and walked out of the bar in defeat.

As soon as they walked out, Dolan walked in with the lady I saw checking him out months ago. She had on a minidress that left little to the imagination and, to be honest, she was more my speed than his.

"Dayum," Greg said. "She's hot as a mofo."

"What the hell? His wife is laid up in the hospital, and he's in here with her?"

"I guess he got daddy's gene after all," Greg said.

I agreed with Greg on that one. *I guess Dolan needed a change of scenery,* I thought as I pushed the reject button on my phone for the tenth time.

"Hold up, G. I'm going outside to take this call."

"Okay."

As soon as I sat in the driver's seat, I called the number back. I knew exactly who it was. University Hospital of Australia. They wanted me so badly that they offered me a position in their institution every month for the past year. But when they heard about the miracle operation I did on Darica, they were even more impressed. My phones were ringing off the hook, from not only them but several other hospitals across the country. They couldn't have come at a worse time. Darica wasn't fully healed, and I didn't know how long it would take for her body to recover. In addition to that, the woman was everything to me, and I wanted to share my life with her and my kids. I didn't care how much they offered me. No amount of money was going to make me leave.

"Hello, Dr. Rogiers." Her Southern drawl captivated and intrigued me. It was hard to believe she lived in the land Down Under.

"Hello, Dr. Maestro. How are you today?"

"I'm wonderful; would be even better if I had you on my team."

"Now is not a good time for my family, Doc. We're kind of having a tragedy."

"Oh. I'm sorry. Is there anything I can help with?"

"Not at the moment. We're just trying to keep it all together."

"I'll be brief. The reason why I'm calling you today is because they told me to up the ante, this time offering you the chief of staff position and any other offer you want to sit on the table."

"Nothing will make me leave right now," I sighed. "My family just can't do without me." The truth of the matter was, I was giving up the greatest position of my career, at the most prestigious hospital in the country, just to stay with Darica. To me, it was a small price to pay.

"Well, I guess you've made up your mind. But if you think of anything, and I do mean anything at all, that would possibly persuade you to come out to UHOA, we will gladly give it to you."

"That's good to know. Thank you, Dr. Maestro."

"You're welcome, Nolan."

Dolan

I almost turned Miko down, especially since she wanted me to ride with her. I didn't fully trust her, but I had to admit, she seemed to be making a lot of strides with her therapy. Her angry demeanor had subsided; she appeared to be monogamous and had even been consistently dating one guy. She'd nixed the supertight miniskirts she wore and replaced them with longer, classier ones. We started out as friends, and I always thought we would be much more, but for some reason, she jumped on my brother first and ended up spending the last decade trying to get back in my good graces. It always ended in disaster. I had no faith that today would be different.

"So, what is it you want me to go to therapy with you for?" I asked.

"If I told you, it wouldn't be a reason for us to have a session," Miko replied. "What I will say is, having you there will dispel some rumors and get us back on track. My therapist wanted me to apologize to people I hurt and confess a secret to them I've kept. I can't think of anyone better to start with than you."

"I'm flattered that you would say that, but do you really think this will help you?"

"I'm not sure, but I'm definitely willing to try."

"I guess it can't hurt."

We had a few more miles to go, but we chose to ride in silence as we listened to old-school music and sang along with the singers. The station was jamming, and we sang and moved to the beat of the music.

"I'm going to slow it down a little bit," the DJ blurted before the previous song even had a chance to finish. "This one's for you, lovers," he said.

Miko didn't recognize the introductory music, but I sure did. I knew it wasn't my car, but I desperately wanted to turn the radio off. Miko reached over and did it for me.

"You don't like that song?" I asked.

"'Endless Love' is one of my favorite songs of all time. But I know you and your wife are going through some issues, and you're probably not in the mood to hear it right now."

"You're pretty good," I told her. "Thank you."

"No problem," she said as she pulled into the parking lot of the clinic. I got out and opened her door for her. She smiled. "Such a gentleman," she whispered as we headed into the building.

"I'm so glad you got him to participate," the therapist exclaimed. "Hello, Dolan, I'm Dr. Ross. Thank you for coming."

"My pleasure," I told her. "You're doing a wonderful job. She even looks different."

"We're trying our best," Dr. Ross added. "Miko, I'll let you tell Dolan the same way you told me in your own words what you'd like to confess to him." Miko nodded and told me her story.

"I was a normal teenager with interests in music, fashion magazines, and boys. Meeting you was the best thing that happened to me. My mother was struggling to make ends meet, and my daddy wasn't around much. Mom worked two jobs to put food on the table, and I was home alone a lot. When I wasn't on the phone with you or Carlena, I was over at one of your houses. One night, I decided to stay home and clean up the house for Mom. She worked so hard, and I just wanted to put a smile on her face. I had just finished the bathroom, and I decided to take a shower to wash some of the sweat off me when I heard a knock at the door. I put on a robe and went to answer it. My friend Ricky was there."

"Hi, Miko. I came over to bring you dinner," he said. I hated people to come over without calling, especially when I was home alone, but it was a nice gesture.

"That's so sweet of you," I said as I devoured the cheeseburger and fries.

"There's nothing I wouldn't do for you," he smiled.

"So, what do you have planned for tomorrow?" I changed the subject.

"Hopefully, spend it with you."

"What do you have in mind?"

"A little foreplay," he answered.

"I like you, Ricky. But it's not that type of party. I'm not ready to have sex."

"Hell if you ain't. I see you flaunting that banging body and staring at me when you think I'm not looking. You know you turn me on."

"I don't know what you're talking about, Ricky. You're a good friend, but I don't want you like that."

"That's not what your body language says."

"I'm sorry if I'm sending you mixed signals, Ricky. But I think you should go. My mom will be home in a minute, and I need to get this house cleaned up." I laughed nervously.

"Bullshit. She won't be home for hours, and I can tell you already cleaned up. This place is spotless. I know the drill because I watch you."

"Watch me? What drill?"

"You get up and go to bed at the same time every day. I know what time you eat and take a shower, and I know *you're ready to get all of this," he said as he unzipped his pants, releasing his bricklike package. I got up to run, but he grabbed me by the hair and yanked me down. He tore my robe off and hurled me on the couch. He held me with one hand and tore my panties off with the other. I bit, scratched, and clawed at him, to no avail. I pulled some of his hair and dug my nails in his skin, drawing blood. "Bitch," he snarled, slapping me so hard, I felt a headache coming on. "You want it rough, don't you, whore?"*

"Ricky, stop. If you leave now, I won't tell."

"You won't tell anyway. I'm getting some of this loving today, and you'll come begging for more. Just calm down, and it'll be easy."

"Whyyyyyyy?"

"You asked for it. You bitches always ask for it."

He grabbed his huge rod and tried to shove it into me. I prayed he wouldn't be able to get it in without lubrication, but he was damn sure trying, and I was in so much pain. Just when I almost gave up, I felt him rise up. Someone had pulled him off me. It was his friend, Kenneth.

"Hey, man. Are you sure everything is okay? I can hear her screaming from outside."

"Damn, man. I didn't get a chance to do anything yet. I thought you were coming to warn me somebody was coming. Some lookout you are. Go back out there and watch out for me."

"I don't know about this, man. I don't think she's feeling you."

"She wants it. Right before you got here, she told me she likes it rough. I was only giving her what she asked for."

"Please—"

"Look at her begging," he lied. "Go back out there. We don't want her mother pulling up on us." Kenneth hesitantly walked back outside, and Ricky took my virginity.

"Why didn't you tell me? I would've beaten his ass," I blurted.

"I couldn't tell a soul. Not even my mother."

"It's very common for a victim to feel guilty, depressed, responsible for the attack, and keep the secret to themselves," Dr. Ross confirmed. "Sometimes, they take it to the grave."

"I'm so sorry that happened to you. But how did you end up with Nolan?"

"That, my friend, has Carlena written all over it. Hold on to your hat," she winked.

"Unfortunately, we're out of time," Dr. Ross interrupted. "Do you think you can come to another session, Dolan?"

"Sure," I told them as we got up to leave. Miko was disappointed, but she agreed to wait.

Chapter Six

Rolonda

It was about one o'clock in the morning, and I couldn't sleep. No matter how many times we changed the locks, beefed up security, and stepped up our alarm system, I still didn't feel comfortable in my huge house. Ever since poor Darica was stabbed, I couldn't help but wonder if our home was really safe. Phillip assured me it was and that he was doing everything in his power to not only find out about the attacker but also to make sure our home was secured. The police had taken the surveillance tapes but had yet to report if they found anything. After tossing and turning and worrying myself to death for another hour, I bolted up out of bed, threw on a robe, and padded downstairs to my kitchen.

I planned on making chicken fettuccine Alfredo for the longest, and, truth be told, cooking was the only thing that calmed my rattled nerves. I grabbed milk, butter, Philadelphia cream, cheddar, and Parmesan cheese out of the refrigerator, and fettuccine noodles out of the cabinet. I rinsed out a pot, filled it with hot water, turned on the burner, put the noodles in, and washed and patted my chicken breasts before sautéing them in a pan of butter and garlic. Greg came in smelling like a brewery.

"Hey, Mom, what are you doing up this time of the morning?"

"I'm cooking because I can't sleep. What are you doing here at this hour?"

"I came to see Chevette."

"You need to leave that girl alone. If she wanted to see you, she would call you."

"She won't even answer the phone."

"Exactly."

"Whose side are you on, Mom? You're helping her, and she's trying to leave me. What if she ends up with someone else?"

"That's probably what she needs to do. I'm not taking sides. You're the one who took the girl through hell and high water. Don't you think she's tired by now?"

"I love her, Mom."

"Then why are we having this conversation?"

"I'm ready, Mom. Ready to be the husband she needs."

"Does she know that, and does she still want you?"

"I don't know."

"Did you ask her?"

"I can't get her to respond to me at all, Ma. I want to be the man she needs, the husband she always wanted, but I can't get her attention."

"Then show her by leaving those other women alone."

"I'm one step ahead of you. I haven't dealt with Rella in weeks. She came to the bar with her mother in tow, and the baby."

"What kind of woman brings a baby to a bar?"

"A stupid and desperate one. I told her to get lost, asked for a DNA test, and told her not to call me unless it's about the baby."

"Good. That's a start, but if that baby is yours, take care of it. If Chevette tells you that she doesn't love you anymore, that she can't see herself with you, I want you to be a man and walk away like I taught you."

"Yes, Ma. But for the record, I've been giving Rella the money directly. She's been using it on herself."

"Typical. That's what happens when you deal with trifling women. We'll come up with a way to buy the clothes and diapers and whatnot without giving her a dime."

He held out his arms to hug me. I grabbed him and embraced him. A single tear fell from his eye, and he sniffled, quickly wiped his face, and made his way to the staircase.

My heart really went out to my stepson, but he had made his bed, and now he was lying in it. I didn't have the heart to tell him that his wife had gone out, so I was hoping that he would turn around and go home, but he went to her room and found that she was not ignoring his knocks. She wasn't there. He didn't say anything to me, just walked downstairs in defeat, kissed me on the cheek, and went out the front door. I prayed for them. I wanted to see them make it, but they had to want it too.

"What are you doing up so early?" Mama C asked.

"I couldn't sleep," I answered abruptly.

"It'll be all right, baby. Our home is safe, and I know Phillip is having state-of-the-art security installed."

"I hope so. I just can't understand why anybody would come in here and stab that woman within an inch of her life."

"Crazy things happen sometimes. But we'll make it with God's help."

"You're right about that," I agreed.

"What are you making?" she asked.

"Chicken fettuccine."

"Sounds great," she said.

I had melted my butter, added a cup of milk, included my cheeses in small dollops, and added a little bit of seasoning. The sauce smelled delicious. My noodles were tender, so I drained them and added them to the homemade Alfredo sauce and chicken.

"This is delicious," Mama said after she helped herself to a taste.

"Thanks, Mama."

"Are you going to bed now?"

"No, I think I'm going to wait up for Chevette."

"Is my grandson okay?"

"He'll be fine."

"Good. Well, thanks for the treat, love. I'm going to get some more sleep."

"Have a good rest, Mama."

"Get some rest too, baby," she said.

I took a seat at the kitchen table, lay my forehead on it, and immediately dozed off.

Brandon 2003

I waited outside an hour for Rolanda's husband, her driver, and a couple of her employees to leave. I had to admit, this was a hell of a setup, and I was proud of Ro. Even though I had knocked her up with not only one but two of my kids and failed to encourage her to get a high school diploma, she bounced back like a queen and made a name for herself. As beautiful as she was, I wasn't surprised when Phillip Rogiers snatched her up, but what I wasn't bargaining for was her falling in love with him so fast. Rolanda was stubborn as all get-out. I guess she got that from her mama. But the woman had instilled a strong work ethic in her, so I had to give her some credit.

Even if she hadn't ended up filthy rich, I knew my sons would be taken care of. She never took me seriously when I said I wanted to see my boys, including Greg, whom she ironically ended up adopting from Landi. But now that they were teenagers, there were a few things I wanted to put on their minds. Let's face it; Rolanda would never have been able to raise a man. I was proud that Phillip was there to fill in the blanks, but there were just some things that a boy needed his father for. Besides, there was a lot of things in the world that a man needed to be prepared for that only his daddy, his own flesh and blood, could teach him.

As big as that house was and the ease at which I was able to get in that bad baby, I was surprised she didn't have more security. I knew when a man was determined, he could do a lot of things, but I never thought it would be that easy for me to breeze on to their property and walk in the kitchen like it was nothing.

I paused when I saw Rolanda. She hadn't changed a bit. She still had childbearing hips, long, natural hair, and smooth, buttery skin. I almost wanted to take her on sight. I had never stopped loving her, never found a woman who could take her place. I kept trying to fill her shoes with all those other women, but they knew as well as I did that it was a lost cause. I wanted her more than I ever let on, and although I had no right to feel this way or think that she would ever have me again, my heart refused to let her go. It was enough I had invaded her privacy and walked in her home uninvited. She hummed a small tune as she finished washing their breakfast dishes, rinsed, then placed them in the dish drain. At that moment, I envied Phillip for being able to come home to this drop-dead gorgeous trophy.

She was about to place the last glass away when something prompted her to turn around, and she saw me. The glass slipped out of her hand, instantly fell on the ground, and shattered in small pieces all over the marble floor.

"Damn you, Brandon. What the hell are you doing in my house?"

"I come in peace," I said as I reached down to help her pick up the broken glass.

"Since when?" she asked as she grabbed a broom and dustpan. "How the hell did you get in here?"

"Don't be so mean, baby. I just came to ask a favor," I smirked. I knew Rolanda like a book. She was angry, scared, and turned on at the same time. At that moment, I could have probably screwed her on the kitchen counter, but I didn't come for that.

"I want to see my sons."

"Humph," she said as if that was the most ludicrous thing I ever suggested. "It's a little late for a pat on the back and a treat. I know you didn't come to offer money. You never spent a dime to take care of them."

"They didn't need it. You have enough money to take care of half the kids in the neighborhood."

"That's beside the point. You didn't even help raise them."

"You honestly think I bought that act that you wanted me to be any kind of force in their lives?"

"So, what do you want with them now, Brandon? I don't have all day."

"Let me have them for winter break."

"Hell no."

"They're almost grown men. Let them decide."

"Let us decide what?" a deep baritone voice said from across the room. I turned around and looked into three faces that mirrored my own. The voice belonged to my oldest son, Nolan. Standing next to him was my youngest son, Dolan, and behind them stood my middle son, Greg.

Dolan

Tonette was incredibly easy to talk to, as if I were talking to an old friend. We laughed, drank more than we should have, then went back to my place to eat and watch movies. When my brothers saw us walk into Massey's, I thought their tongues would fall out of their mouths. I must have been a sight to see. Just a few months ago, I was shaking my head at their horny asses, and all I wanted to do was be a good husband and father. Now, I had a honey on my arm that I'd be a fool not to bang.

Tonette and I fell asleep on the couch together, and when we woke up, it was like we both forgot that we weren't a couple. She started kissing me. It felt good to be touched for a change. Don't get me wrong. I could've had sex with her, but I didn't want to do that just yet. I wanted Tonette on my own terms. I had caused Darica enough heartache and pain, and this was where I drew the line. I felt I owed her a chance to have her say before I stepped out.

I helped Tonette to her feet, and she was a little disoriented. I was glad we didn't make love. I didn't want to take advantage of a woman who had too much to drink, and I was sure she wouldn't feel good about herself in the morning. I made her a bed on the couch because I didn't want to put her in my wife's bed, nor did I want her in the guest room. I didn't want her to be attached like that. She was a nice woman, and I planned to be her friend for as long as I could. I wanted to take care of my business before I moved forward in my life. I knew my wife had cheated, but it didn't stop me from loving her or doing the right thing.

Darica was the only thing on my mind lately. I knew I needed to visit her. She would need a lot of support when she came home from the hospital, but to be perfectly honest, I didn't know if we would be able to live under the same roof. By the time I got up the next morning, Tonette was gone. She left a note for me.

Thanks for last night. I had a blast.
Tonette.
P.S. Thanks for being a real man.

I knew exactly what she meant, and I smiled. I took my shower, got dressed, grabbed my keys, and headed for the hospital to have a conversation with my wife. When I arrived, Nolan was comfortably sitting in her room. He didn't look too happy to see me, but Darica seemed glad. She was eating some ice cream I know he bought her. I greeted my brother, but he knew as well as I did that I wasn't up to talking to him. That's why I ignored his calls. Who knows, maybe if I had, I would have found out some interesting information. But right now, I had to get my priorities in order, and talking to my wife was the first thing on the list. Nolan excused himself, and I sat on the edge of Darica's bed.

"So, how are you feeling?" I asked her.

"Okay, I can't complain," she said. She looked a little uneasy, as if I had surprised her or caught her with her hand in the cookie jar. Nevertheless, I cut right to the chase.

"Darica, did you cheat on me?" I asked my wife. She looked like she wanted to crawl up under a rock, but the expression on her face told me she wouldn't protest because she knew I knew her long enough to know when she was lying.

"Where did you get that information?"

"I went on the clinic's website; then I called them because I was puzzled about something. I found out that the treatments really didn't work." I didn't bother to tell her about the doctor I went to for a second opinion. Darica swallowed the lump in her throat and went to speak, but no words came out. "I know for a fact you cheated on me," I said. Tears started rolling down her face.

"Who is your source?" she asked through sniffles.

"I'm not ready to reveal that right now," I lied. "But I hope you're ready to reveal who you cheated on me with."

"It was a one-night stand, and it wasn't important. It just happened. Your turn," she had the nerve to say. I couldn't believe I was sitting here playing tit-for-tat with Darica. She knew I wasn't about games.

"I told you it was Carlena, and she really didn't mean anything to me," I said. "So, now that the secret is out, what do we do?"

"I think we need to cool it for a while."

"What about the baby?" I asked.

"I don't think you want the responsibility."

"You're right. Not under these circumstances," I said more out of anger than anything else. Darica's mouth dropped open so wide that I thought it was going to fall on the bed. With that, I got up, walked away, and didn't look back.

Nolan

I channel surfed for about thirty minutes, but there was nothing on TV. It was times like these that made me question what I was thinking when I bought this huge house. It was so big that people's voices echoed off the walls when they talked. For a fleeting moment, I wondered how screams of passion would sound bouncing off them, then settled on a blaring soap opera, and threw the remote on the couch. Some woman was screaming about her undying love to some player. What a hell of a way to spend my day.

I went up to the hospital to see Darica earlier, grabbed both of her hands, and was on the verge of telling her the story about Sheila, Ari, and the night she first met me, when Dolan showed up at the hospital unannounced. I knew she thought Dolan saved her, but I wasn't sure if Dolan really stole her from me, so I was going to come clean about that too. I figured we'd compare notes and come up with something, but I didn't know exactly what outcome I actually expected. When he came in like gangbusters, as much as I hated to, I had to bow out and allow him to talk to his wife.

I stood at the doorway and watched them awhile. They looked so perfect together, and a small part of me wanted to let them be. But every time I tried, my heart would skip a beat, my mouth would dry out, and the thought of leaving her felt like I was dying a slow death. I never meant for any of this to happen. I just wanted to reconcile with my brother and maybe get back in my sister-in-law's good graces, but things didn't go at all as I planned. The child we set out to create actually manifested, no matter how selfish it was of us to bring it into our drama-filled world. Funny how things never end the way they start.

Nevertheless, I was excited about the baby, wanted it more than anything, and I wanted the mother even more than that. I couldn't imagine living my life without her, and I was prepared to tell my mother, father, Evette, and the world that she was the woman I wanted to spend the rest of my life with. Nurse Ratchet was blowing me up, so I decided to call her and see what time she wanted to meet. I had to put out that fire first.

When Nurse R arrived at the hotel room, I was impressed. She was a halfway decent-looking woman outside of her work clothes. She had on a tight minidress, but it was tasteful; her face was made up, and she had taken down her bun, let her hair hang loose, and had even invested in a manicure and pedicure. I allowed her to go in first, while I made a few phone calls. She was in there all of three minutes when I got a text from her telling me to hurry up. She was a nervous wreck.

"I'm sorry about this. I feel so ashamed," she said.

"It's cool. You know what you want, and you're all about your business. I guess we should get right to it."

"I guess so."

"No offense, but what's a nice girl like you doing in a place like this?"

"I've fantasized about you forever. I just thought it would be nice."

"OK."

"Do you love her?"

"I'd rather not say."

"I'm sorry. I'm prying."

"Yes, you are."

"Can you hold me?"

"Sure."

She was silent for a while, so I took the opportunity to pour us a glass of wine. She drank a few glasses and started undressing me. She looked at my body like she had never been with a man. So, I asked her.

"Have you ever been with a man?"

"I've never been with a man like you," she said.

"I'm flattered," I said as I started to undress her. She was shaking. "Don't be nervous."

"OK."

I put on a condom and reached over to put her hand on my abs, and she trembled. I maneuvered her in the missionary position so that she could get a glimpse of my whole body. Her teeth were chattering.

"It's okay. We'll go slowly."

"OK," she said, bracing herself like I was about to pull out her teeth. As soon as I tried to penetrate her . . . She passed out.

"Now, that's a first," I said.

I got up, grabbed her phone, then took my own phones out of my pocket, and went into the bathroom to call Litha.

"I have the phone and all the information you need," I said.

"Good. Give us a minute, and we'll deactivate the account and find out if she forwarded anything to another device." I held the line until she came back with the confirmation. "All clear but destroy that phone and the burner phone you have, just in case."

"My sentiments exactly," I told her. I got dressed, gulped my glass of wine, and said a silent goodbye to Nurse Ratchet. "You ain't ready, love," I chuckled as I made my way to my car to destroy the evidence.

Darica

What do you do when your husband confronts you, accuses you of sleeping with another man, looks at you like he wants to kill you, and tells you he's done? Do you confide in him, come clean, tell him you didn't mean it, blame it on your hormones, and your lack of affection, your selfishness? Do you tell him you're sorry you were having his brother's baby, not because you decided to make him a donor, but because you were too self-centered to think it through?

I wanted to be angry at them for coming up with that stupid plan, but the truth was, I wanted it more than they did. Nobody forced me to jump in Nolan's bed like a deprived sex addict and let him have me every which way he chose. No. I did that all by myself, and now I had to face the music, knowing it would only be a matter of time before someone told Dolan I slept with Nolan, or he'd put two and two together and figure it out on his own. I saw the way Nolan was acting, and my greatest fear was *he'd* be the one to blow it. I'd tried to hide my indiscretions, tried to sweep them under the rug that was too small for the floor, tried to pretend I lived in a perfect bubble, but when it shattered, I was lost, helpless, hopeless, and didn't know what to do.

They were sending me to rehab instead of home, a place I would normally refuse if not for the fact I was afraid I might not have a home to go to. Maybe when I came out, I would be able to think more clearly, because right now, I was a basket case thinking about all the things I wanted: to be happy about my pregnancy, to shout it to the world. Instead, I thought about getting rid of my child, the thing I was so proud of, yet couldn't enjoy now.

I wanted peace of mind, to enjoy my good man, to not be so disgusted with myself, to feel like I deserved him; when, in fact, I wasn't good enough for him. He deserved a woman who could love him better—anybody but Carlena. I despised her ass and wanted to kick the shit out of her. She had caused so many problems in my life, and I was having so many nightmares about my near-death experience that all I could think about was getting revenge. I wanted to leave town again but thought it best to face my problems head-on. I wanted to get a hotel room but didn't have money to pay for it or anyone to take care of my injuries. A home health nurse would only be assigned for a few hours, and my handful of family and friends had lives of their own. I knew that being a caregiver wasn't exactly at the top of their list.

I had to be honest with myself. If I had thought about my wants instead of my needs, I wouldn't be in this predicament. My situation was stressful, but not half as much as it would be if I kept kicking myself about it. So, I decided to give myself a break, closed my eyes, and rested my head on my pillow. Suddenly, I heard footsteps; I wasn't expecting any visitors, but that didn't stop the trio that came into my room. That was the trouble with hospitals. People were allowed to show up with no warning, regardless if you wanted to see them or not. When they walked in, I adjusted myself in the hospital bed, rolled my eyes, grabbed the call button, and pushed it like I was losing my mind.

"May I help you?" someone at the nurse's station asked.

"Doesn't the hospital have a policy against too many damn people coming up at one to time to visit a patient?"

"Ma'am, if you're talking about the three visitors I just watched walk into your room, that's a sufficient amount."

"Not in my book," I looked at them all and said.

"Baby, don't be like that," my mother spoke.

What a lot of people didn't know was the person I referred to as my mother was not really my mother. Technically, she was my aunt. I went to live with her shortly after I was attacked. I could never bring myself to go back and live with my real mother after what happened with Ben. I felt sorry for him, and I wanted him to be acquitted, but at the same time, I was angry at him for being a crackhead and allowing me to be put in a predicament of almost being raped. The former champ found out I was in the hospital and decided to visit me. The last person I wanted to see was that bastard. The second to the last person I wanted to see was my real mother. But I never thought both of them would be visiting me at the same time and bring in Ben as an added bonus.

I didn't know what made me madder. The fact that this desperate, money-grubbing, low-life bitch had accepted her drug-addicted, no-money-having, on-the-street-begging, poor excuse for a man after he allowed me to get attacked in an alley, or the fact that she had forgiven this washed up, wannabe celebrity, block face, so-called redeemed rapist. They were all standing there smiling at me like I just told them I'd won a million-dollar lottery, and I hated every one of them. I started hollering and screaming bloody murder, hoping someone would come in and save me from this nightmare when Nolan walked in.

"Hey, hey, what's going on?" he said.

"These people are disturbing me."

"I'm sure you guys know the rules against upsetting the patients. I'll have to ask you to leave the hospital."

"We haven't said two words to her," my mother said. "I'm her *real* mother," she said, extending her hand to Nolan.

"Oh, wow. Now I see where Darica gets her good looks," he said, instantly getting pulled into her web.

"This is my husband, Ben, Darica's stepfather, and, of course, you know the champ."

"Yes, yes. So nice of you to come. I'll let you visit in peace."

Ain't this some shit. I shook my head. Even Nolan couldn't resist the charming Miss Ross. I watched him walk out of the hospital room as if nothing ever happened.

"How are you feeling, dear?" my mother asked. But before I could answer, she spoke again. "When I heard of your accident, I wanted to come right then and there, but I knew that would be a problem since you're not answering any of my calls."

"It wasn't an 'accident'; it was an assault. I haven't seen you since you took *him* back." I nodded my head toward Ben.

"I thought you were good with it. You were the one who said justice should be done."

"I've been clean for ten years," he chimed in. "I want to make amends. I need your forgiveness and for you to accept me."

"Don't you think it's a little late to play daddy?" I spat. Ben just closed his eyes and shook his head. The champ stepped forward. I was wondering when his coward ass was going to speak.

"Darica, I just want to say I'm so sorry about what I did to you."

I spat in his face. "Don't talk to me about 'sorry.' You treated me like a ho on the street, and if Ben hadn't stopped you, you probably would have taken my virginity and gotten me pregnant."

"But nothing happened. So, can we be friends?"

"You may be able to pay off Bonnie and Clyde here, but nothing you do will ever change what you did to me. Now, get the hell out of my face."

Chapter Seven

Nurse Ratchet/Lala

I walked into the run-down diner exhausted. My head was hurting, my feet were killing me, and my back was screaming from lifting patients.

"Can I get you anything?" the waitress asked.

"Just coffee," I said as I rubbed my temples.

The place was old, the tables wobbly, and the tiles on the floor were cracked, but it was clean, and the grade on the window said "A." I thought about ordering something to eat, but I changed my mind when I thought about all the food I had at home. The detective was late as usual, and I knew I'd go through two cups of coffee and an orange juice before he even graced the parking lot.

Late ass, I thought when I saw his beat-up Tahoe pull up. I was so full of sugar by then that I was shaking like a hand mixer.

"Sorry I'm late," he said. "Any news?"

"If you're asking me how my day was at the hospital, it was fucked-up. The management is ungrateful, and all the patients do is complain."

"You still haven't learned the ropes, I see."

"This is the first job that I can't get into. The last one was easy. I was a stripper and took to the pole like I was born to do it. The job before that, I was a teacher, and that was a piece of cake too. This shit here is for the birds."

"You might consider taking a few classes. We need to crack down on this fraud at Lake and nail that killer. Don't think I missed that shit you pulled with that surgeon."

"Nothing happened, if that's what you want to know. I passed out before he could do anything. Anyway, he's clean, not abusing any patients. He's just sprung by one, in particular, somebody he knew already. Apparently, she was stabbed in a closet at his mother's house, and he saved her life."

"Aww. Ain't that special. Take those classes and get on your job, Ratchet."

"How do you know about that nickname?"

"Hospital buzz."

I handed Detective Hughes a mint. He took it, unwrapped it, placed it in his mouth, sucked on it, and made my life better. I was always his friend and probably would always be. I didn't mince words with him, and I told him he needed to take care of himself. He used to be fine, I mean drop-dead gorgeous, a fresh dresser, good head of hair, and kept up with his hygiene. The job ate him up, reduced him to somebody he was not and made him into an obsessed freak that no one wanted to be bothered with.

"You need to reevaluate yourself," I told him.

"I know. I have an appointment with the dentist for gum surgery."

"Good. With a job like yours, you need to get your act together."

"You don't have to tell me twice. I know what it takes to be a success. It's just that this case is—"

"This case is going to be fine," I interrupted. "We're going to crack it wide open, find that killer, and turn that hospital's reputation around. We have to." He nodded in agreement and breathed a sigh of relief. I was glad to see he still had faith in me.

"I finally got around to reviewing those surveillance cameras."

"Good. What'd you come up with?"

"I saw a suspicious-looking maid run through the house. She had what looked like blood on her uniform right before she disappeared from camera coverage. I'm trying to locate her name and whereabouts from the home owners."

"That sounds promising."

"Yeah. I hope so."

"Did you get DNA samples from the crime scene?"

"Yep."

"Did you get a statement from the victim?"

"Yes, but she didn't remember anything."

"Oh."

"Where are you headed tonight, Lala?" he asked, finally addressing me by my real name.

"Home. Want to come?" I was hoping he said no, not because I didn't enjoy his company but because I needed more from a man. I think that's probably why I latched on to Nolan. He represented everything I wanted, and I desperately needed physical contact with the opposite sex, but I needed Hughes to realize I meant business. I wanted the man he *used* to be. It wasn't fair to Nolan that I hopelessly pushed myself on him, knowing he was too rich for my poor self-esteem. It was all a dream.

"Not tonight. I have to meet with an old friend. We'll meet up again soon."

"Okay. I'll see you later."

"Bye."

I took a walk down Main Street, hung a left, and ended up at my sister Litha's house. She wasn't home, so I climbed in through her window. Her television was blaring. She always kept it on, along with all the lights. If her place was going to get robbed, she was going to make sure they did the guesswork on if anyone was home or not. I found a pitcher of Kool-Aid in the fridge and poured me a large glass, then went into the den to watch a movie until I heard her put her key in the door.

"Hey, sis," she greeted me.

"Hey, yourself," I shot back. "You still mad at me?"

"No. I just wish we were more alike."

"It's not my fault you choose to be on the opposite side of the law."

"I want to help those in need. At least, I'm up front about it."

"Working law enforcement has its perks."

"Not when it dupes hardworking people."

"You must mean Nolan."

"Exactly. He's a good man. Just in love with a woman."

"I figured as much."

"So, you'll let him make it?"

"Yes, sis."

"Cool. You hungry."

"Yeah. I could eat."

Rolanda 2003

I could not believe Brandon's ass was standing inside my home, asking me if he could take my babies over to his house. Christmas had just rolled around, and his ass didn't even bother to send them a card. Over the years, I'd taken care of the boys, and it was no secret that I had enough money to do so, but what gave this bastard the right to invade my privacy, come up in my house, and ask if he could take anybody's kids? He was the most unfit motherfucking father I had ever seen in my life, and I didn't want my children to have any part of him. If Landi herself came here and gave him permission to take Greg,

I would've kicked both their asses out on their ear. I was still trying to figure out how he got past security.

"Please don't be mad at me, Rolanda," Brandon begged. "I've been watching the boys go to and from school for the past five years. I'll admit that I wasn't the man or the father that I needed to be. I was stuck on some dumb shit, but I knew you were doing good for yourself, and marrying Phillip was the best move by far. I can't take anything from the man. He raised my boys up to this point, and I'm never going to try to be him. But I do want my sons to know me and feel like I'm a part of their lives. Christmas just passed, and I not only bought them gifts, but I've also been buying gifts for the past five years. I realized I missed out on a lot, but I want to start doing things like play basketball and go to the movies with them."

"Don't you think it's a little late to start playing daddy?"

"It's never too late," he said.

He looked over at all three of his children, scared to death at what they would say. The expressions on their faces weren't easy to read, but if I could take a guess, I would say they were willing to accept their father. They had pretty open minds.

"Well, what do you think, kids?"

"Sure," they all said in unison.

"Then it's settled. When do you want to go over to your father's house?" I asked them. They all hunched their shoulders, so Brandon spoke up.

"I was thinking maybe New Year's Eve. I'm not doing much of anything that night, so that would be a perfect night. That way, we can bring in the New Year together. I think it's a sign of good luck."

"I think that's a great idea, but let me talk to Phillip. I'll, of course, leave the part out about you *sneaking* into this house, and I'll get back with you."

"Great," Brandon said as he went over to grab his boys into a group hug. All seemed great. I just hoped Phillip would see it that way. I crossed my fingers as Brandon walked out and got into his car.

Dolan

I was always levelheaded. Even when we took our first trip over to our dad's house after he begged Mom to let us visit him, I had to take the reins because Nolan and Greg clearly went over the deep end. Daddy was one of the coolest cats we'd ever seen, so it wasn't surprising when we saw the way he had his crib set up. It was a two-story tract house with mission tile and all the amenities in a nice little neighborhood. He had his living room decked out with the fanciest furniture, and his kitchen full of state-of-the-art appliances. His friend, Steven, was there. They apparently were both bachelors, and Steven was his roommate.

"What's up, little homie?" Steven said. "Good to finally see you again."

"Again?" I asked.

"I haven't seen you little soldiers since you were crawling on the floor."

"Cool," Nolan said. "So, I guess you're like my dad's best friend?"

"You could say that," he confirmed. "I've been knowing his ugly ass since forever. So, how long will you guys be staying with us?"

"I don't know," Greg told him. "We're going to bring in the New Year with him and go from there."

"That's all right," he said as the house phone started ringing. Our dad got a business call, something about a sanitation emergency, whatever that was, and he had to leave right away.

"Hopefully, I'll be back before the countdown," he said. "You guys make yourself at home."

Nolan and Greg went into the den where there was a big-screen TV, a stereo, and all kinds of games a teenager could get lost in. Loads of full liquor bottles lined the cabinets on the walls. I only drank alcohol when Mom and Dad allowed us to have a couple of sips of wine, but that wasn't very often. Nolan tried to gulp down the whole damn bar.

"Slow down, man. You don't want to be toasted when Dad comes back. You're going to get us in trouble," I told him.

"It's not like he can beat our ass or nothing. He just came back in the picture," Nolan said as he noticed Greg trying to work the game.

"Give me that, you little dummy. You don't know how to play," he said as he yanked the controller out of Greg's hands.

"I'll beat your ass any day," Greg told him.

"Hey, watch your mouth," I said.

"You ain't that much older than me," he retorted. A few hours later, we saw people, mostly women, coming into the house. Apparently, Dad was having a party and forgot to tell us.

"What's going on?" Nolan asked.

"I invited a couple of chickenheads over here," Steven said.

"Damn, they're fine."

"That's the only kind of women I deal with," Steve told us. "See for yourself." He pointed.

The next thing we knew, about ten women with banging bodies and next to no clothes on walked in, sat in the living room, and helped themselves to drinks.

"Are all of them for you?" Nolan asked.

"They don't have to be," Steve said. "You can have one of them if you can handle it."

"Thanks, man," Nolan said.

"What are you doing?" I asked him. "You don't know nothing about women."

"I know about ass and titties," he smiled.

I took Greg back into the den where I thought he was "safe" and stayed in there with him until I heard noises. I opened the door to check out what was going on in the hallway. The woman standing there immediately caught my attention. It was Mia from third grade. The only thing that reminded me it was her was her face. Her chest had grown considerably, her waist had shrunk, and her ass looked like an onion. If that wasn't enough, her beautiful eyes were even more breathtaking than they were when we were kids.

"Oh my God. What are you doing here?" she asked.

"My dad lives here."

"Is Steve your dad?"

"No. Brandon is," I said. "What are *you* doing here?" I asked.

"I'm here on business."

"Really? May I ask what kind of business?" Her smile left, and her whole demeanor changed when she saw Steve.

"Look, I'm not going to sugarcoat shit. I'm an escort, and Steve's kind of, sort of, my boss."

"What?" I said in disbelief.

"Look, I'm sorry to reunite with you under these circumstances, but it is what it is. If you knew my story, you wouldn't judge me."

"I'm not judging, but you had so many other alternatives. You don't have to be on the streets like this."

"I'm *not* on the streets. Steve runs a service where I meet men, and if I want to sex somebody for money,

I do it. If not, we just talk. But either way, they're paying. Which one do you want right now?"

"I'd like to talk to you, but I'm not paying you to do it."

"Then I guess it's the other." She smiled and reached out for me.

"No, it's *not* the other!" I yelled as I pushed her away. "I don't want to fuck you, Mia. I want to be your friend."

"I stopped believing in friendships a long time ago."

"Fine," I said. "I don't want you to miss any money, so you go on about your business. It was good seeing you either way."

"Likewise," she said as she walked away.

Like I said, I've always been the rational one. Our trip to Daddy's house wasn't what we expected, but we rolled with the punches. At least, I did. But, that's more than I could say for Nolan and Greg. That's another story for another day. Right now, my rationale was about to walk right out the door. I was sick and tired of being the man I was and getting nothing for it.

Yes, I had found a good wife, but she chose someone else. Yes, I had gotten played by a doctor that for whatever sick reason chose to sterilize me temporarily. But I was a good husband, and my wife didn't have to do what she did. To tell the truth, I was still deeply in love with her. She was my everything; my first love, my every breath, and every step that I made. My whole life revolved around Darica, and I didn't have any regrets. I'd made a few mistakes along the way, but I corrected them. But, as always, I got shitted on. So, you know what? It was high time for me to let that life go. No more Darica, no more Mr. Nice. Just good, clean fun. I picked up the phone and dialed Tonette's number. She was saying she wanted to move on to the next level, so I told her to prepare for a night of passion—something she probably never had experienced and never would again.

Nolan

Thinking about my brother and the fucked-up position we found ourselves in had me sifting through all the stuff we went through over the years. Nothing stood out more than the day our dad brought us to his home to "bond." Unfortunately, he had to go to work that day, and things went a little awry. I was always the fast one and didn't have any regrets about it. Even back then, when I was a virgin, I was off the chain. I loved to see women in porn, and I took every opportunity to watch it.

When Steve invited the X-rated women in the house, I thought I was in hooker heaven with a front seat at an up close and personal event. When one of them started flirting with me, I felt like the luckiest man in the world. I knew I was young and probably couldn't last two minutes with her. But the stuff she said and did really blew my mind.

"Hey, baby, want to play a game?"

"Hell yeah."

"How much money do you have?"

"About fifty dollars."

"A lot could happen with that kind of money."

"Like what?" I asked her.

"Like this," she said, taking off the scarf from around her waist and tying it around my eyes.

"I like this game already," I told her.

"You want to take it further?" she asked.

"Yes, ma'am," I said as I pulled the twenties out of my pocket and hoped I gave her the right amount because I couldn't see with the blindfold on. When I heard her purr, I knew she was happy with the money, and she proceeded to unzip my pants. The next thing I knew, she was working my little man like it was going out of style. I couldn't believe the shit she was doing to me with her tongue, and my little brain saw fireworks. This was better than anything I had ever seen on cable because it was physically happening to me. I was about to be introduced to lovemaking by a pro, something I never thought I would do, and I didn't even care. Right now, I was about to become a man, and I didn't even have to plan for it. After she tasted me and I surprisingly didn't explode in her mouth, she straddled me. It was pure heaven. She rode me like a race horse, and I almost died from the pleasure.

The next thing I knew, she ripped the blindfold off during my release. I couldn't believe my eyes. I was staring at my crush from third grade . . . Mia. The original prostitute must have left the room after she blindfolded me, and Mia came in to take her place. This was a far cry from grade school. She was a full-grown, beautiful, sexy, badass woman. The reunion would have been bittersweet if not for the fact Dolan busted in the room at that moment. We barely had time to recognize each other, but Dolan took one look at us and crossed the room to beat the shit out of me.

By the time Mom got to Dad's house, Dolan and I were in a full-fledged fight. Greg called her when he saw the scene, put two and two together, and couldn't break us up. Unfortunately, Daddy did not know of it until several hours later. My mom called him everything but a child of God and vowed never to let us come over to his house again. Brandon swore that he had nothing to do with it, that Steve had mixed business with pleasure by inviting the ladies of the night and a few good men to the house, hoping to make some quick cash. But she wasn't buying the story. She was convinced Brandon was trying to make up for lost time by schooling his sons to make them pimps. In her eyes, he had exposed her babies to the ultimate sin. Dolan was convinced I was an asshole who

didn't care about anybody but myself, Greg thought we
had lost our marbles, and none of us had any idea what
impact that night would mean in our lives.

Chapter Eight

Dolan

When I arrived at Tonette's house to pick her up, she kept me waiting at her door for over fifteen minutes. I kept shifting from side to side, wondering if she was ever going to come outside, but when she did, it was well worth it.

She had on a beautiful, purple sequin Armani cocktail dress that stopped smack in the middle of her thick thighs. Her hair was swept in a bun with tendrils of curls cascading her face, which was lightly made up with lipstick the color of her dress and a little eyeliner and mascara. Her bright complexion was flawless.

She gave me the once-over and a nod of approval. I was clean shaven with a grey Armani suit and eggplant tie. It was like we had coordinated our attire. I had neatly trimmed my beard because I was trying to let it grow out. I reached out my arm for her to grab and escorted her to the car.

"Where are we going tonight?" she asked.

"To a little cafe by the ocean. You do like surf and turf, right?"

"Of course."

Tonette was quiet during the drive to the restaurant, but she did hold my hand as I drove. She even felt me up a few times, which told me she liked what was there. I smiled and let her have her feel.

When we got to the restaurant, I almost turned and
went back to my car. I saw Chevette coming out with
her friend, who happened to have the same name as my
brother, Greg, only his was spelled with two *g*'s. I didn't
know who was more ashamed, her or me, but what I
did know was she was going to give Darica an earful
first chance she got. I gave her a look that said, please,
believe me, baby. I'm gonna do the same.

I grabbed Tonette's elbow and escorted her inside
the restaurant where we were immediately seated. The
waitress came to take our order, and Tonette allowed me
to choose her meal. We both had the filet mignon with
sautéed shrimp and new potatoes, which we devoured
with several glasses of red wine before polishing off two
orders of Crème Brûlée. When we were nice and full, I
paid the check and escorted her back to the car.

"So, what do you want to do now?" I asked.

"Fuck," she said, catching me by surprise.

"Okay," I said, making a quick right on two wheels to
get to the Sheraton.

Once we were inside our room, I jumped in the shower, while she made herself more comfortable. When I
came out in a towel, she started kissing me and quickly
removed it, leaving me completely naked. To be honest,
I wasn't feeling her like that. I was still in Darica mode,
and she was the only woman I wanted to sleep with. But
I knew I needed to move forward at some point, and now
was as good a time as any. Besides, I'd have to be deaf,
dumb, and blind not to appreciate the naked beauty in
front of me. At this moment, I recalled the only visual
enhancement I could think of, which was a movie I saw
of a woman sexing two men in 2007. I blocked them
out, of course, and helped Tonette straddle me just like
I saw the woman do in the movie. Her love tunnel was
hot and tight, gripping my enraged manhood like a vice.

We bumped and grinded like it was our last time, and just as she was ready to tap out, I turned her over on her stomach and entered her from the back. Her moans were so animalistic and wild that the neighbors started beating on the walls. I was guessing they didn't appreciate the high-pitched assault on their ears. But I sure did because they were music to mine.

"Damn, Dolan. You are beating it up."

"Shut up and take it," I said as I slapped her ass.

"Damn, baby. Go easy on me, please."

"I'm giving you what you wanted," I reminded her.

"I can't lie. I love a man who's not afraid to put it on me."

"I know."

"But I can't take it."

"Too damn bad," I told her. She kept looking at me in disbelief. I didn't blame her. I surprised myself. The feeling was so intense that I started coming.

"Aaaah, shit," I said as I pulled out, yanked off the condom, and let my seeds fall on her onion ass. She rolled over and looked at me like I was somebody else. I knew I was changing because I felt it too. I watched her calm her heavy breathing and close her eyes. Seconds later, she was snoring.

Darica

When Dolan called and told me he was taking me to the rehab center, I was ecstatic. I took it as a sign that he wanted to make things work. I needed Dolan in my life, had never been separated from him in the five years we were married, and this was starting to get unbearable. It was easy for me to wash now, and with a mirror, I could make myself look halfway decent. I did a quick sponge bath, then put on the dress my so-called mother had brought me trying to get back in my good graces, and put my hair in a messy bun. I pulled my purse out of the drawer and found my makeup, beat my face as best I could, and was ready just in time to see Dolan walk in the door. The smile on his face told me that I'd done a good job. I was hoping we would have a good day.

My nurse brought in a wheelchair, and Dolan reached under my armpits so he could help me transfer into it from the bed. It felt so good to be in his arms. I didn't know how to act and held on a little longer than I should have. I kept making little remarks, trying to flirt with him while hoping to get some semblance of what we used to have. But Dolan wasn't budging. I mean, I know I made my bed, and now I had to lie in it, but it damn sure wasn't any easier to deal with. Dolan shrugged me off, treating me like I were a stranger off the street but remained cordial as he wheeled me out of the hospital and into the parking lot.

We made small talk as he drove to the rehab center. So many times I wanted to tell him the truth—just throw everything out there and let him know that I loved him, and I wanted to try to work it out despite what happened . . . to let him know I loved him so much I'd do anything in my power to make our marriage work. But I knew that it was probably not going to be well received, and he would probably send me packing either way. So, I decided not to say anything just yet. I allowed him to drive me to the rehab center, make sure I got acquainted with my new surroundings, and leave.

It broke my heart to watch him walk out the door. He took one last look at me like it would definitely be our last time seeing each other. I looked for a glimmer of hope, something to let me know that sooner or later we'd get back together, but what I saw scared the hell out of me.

It was a new Dolan, a changed man . . . A man I'd never seen before . . . A confident, cocky man, a man who didn't want or need me, a man who knew he wanted more than just his wife to fill his needs, a man who would fuck somebody else in a heartbeat—and probably already did. He kissed me on the cheek and walked away, taking my heart with him. As soon as Dolan left, Chevette came in.

"Hey, girl. If I'd known you were coming, I would've had you pick me up from the hospital instead of Dolan," I told her.

"That was sweet of him. Hopefully, you guys can get back together soon. I know he was happy to see you," she said.

"Not this time, honey. Dolan looks like he's moved on."

"Maybe he's just trying to do something to pass the time."

"Chevette, what are you talking about?"

"Maybe he's just testing the waters."

"You know something, don't you?"

"No."

"Chevette?"

"I'm probably wrong."

"What happened?"

"It was nothing. Nothing at all."

"Can you tell me something about this 'nothing'?"

"I was coming out of a café, and I saw Dolan with a young lady."

"What?"

"He probably just met her while he was waiting to eat dinner or something. Maybe it was his coworker."

"How were they dressed?"

"They both wore purple."

"That's no coincidence. How did she look?"

"She was okay."

"Chevette, don't sugarcoat it. Were they on a date or not?"

"It looked like they were," she reluctantly admitted. "Why are you badgering me about this?"

"Because I want to know if she's the woman that's taking Dolan's heart."

"All you have to do is tell him what it is that you're keeping from him so you guys can get back together. How hard is that?"

"Don't be funny. You know there are certain things I can't talk to Dolan about."

"Well, tell me what it is. I'll tell him for you."

"I'm not ready."

"To hell with your secretive ass. Anyway, he saw me with the other Gregg, and I know he's going to tell my husband, but I don't care because I'm filing for divorce. I'm finally ready."

"I never thought I'd be hearing you say that."

"And I never thought you'd be silly enough to lose your husband. Dolan is a good man."

"You don't understand, Chevette."

"What *you* don't understand is, no matter what you tell him, he'll still love you. Just keep it real."

"Dolan is a good man, but sometimes, people just can't work out their differences."

"Fine if you want to sit there and lose a good man over some foolishness, go right ahead. That's almost as insane as staying with a bad one. I'm filing for divorce, and there's nothing we can do about it."

"Are you sure you want to do that? I heard Greg did a one-eighty."

"He's a day late and a dollar short. He should've done it a long time ago."

"I guess you made up your mind."

"I heard Nolan did one as well," she said, ignoring my statement.

"You can't believe everything you hear, although I'm curious to know where you heard it."

"It's obvious. He's not messing around, he doesn't have any women friends, and, to be perfectly honest, he'd rather sit here with you and watch you slowly recover than play around with the hoes he's normally with."

"Stop."

"No, *you* stop. I think Nolan's in love with you, and that's dangerous, considering he's your brother-in-law."

"Nolan and I are just friends. That's all it will ever be."

"Tell it to his heart."

"Speak of the devil," I said when I saw him look in, then walk right back out because he didn't want to invade on our privacy. I prayed he didn't hear any of our conversation.

"Come on in!" Chevette yelled. "I was just leaving. Have a nice day," she said as she kissed my forehead. "I'll call you a little bit later, love."

"Okay."

As soon as she walked out of the room, Nolan walked in.

"Hey, beautiful. How are you feeling?"

"A little better. I'm not having as much pain, and I can do a bit more for myself. I never liked depending on nurses or anybody, for that matter."

"Good. Listen, I just want to talk to you for a second."

"Nolan, I'm grateful for what you did for me, but we can't go on like this. I mean, I'm a married woman."

"A married woman who's separated from her husband. Yeah, I know all about that." I gave him a look of surprise, wondering how he found out so fast.

"I'm *still* a married woman, and even if I weren't promised to your brother, it would be damn near impossible for us to have an affair."

"That's where you're wrong, sweetheart. I don't want to have an affair with you. I want you to be my wife. I know it sounds insane, and it's probably the stupidest thing I've ever said, but you've changed me. I can't be with any other women. I don't want to look at one, don't want to talk to one, don't want to feel one, and don't want to fuck one. I just want you."

"I'm glad you finally saw the light, but I can't be that woman. Find someone else."

"There's never going to be another you. Think about what I said, sweets." It was a nickname he used for me.

"There's nothing to think about, Nolan. It's not up for discussion. All we can be is friends. You need to move on."

"I'll leave it alone for now. But either way, we need to tell your husband what we did."

"*What? You're* the main one that didn't want to tell him."

"The secret is eating me up."

"Now you want to get a conscience? You *have* changed. Either that or you bumped your head. What do we look like confessing to him? He'll never understand."

"We have to try. It was wrong, and we have to make it right."

"I can't do this."

"We can't bring a child into the world with all these lies, sweets. We have to come clean."

"What if the child doesn't make it?"

"What the hell do you mean? You have a clean bill of health. The baby is fine."

"What if I change my mind about having it?"

"That's crazy. What are you, suicidal or something? You talking about killing yourself?"

"I want to get an abortion."

"Say *what?*"

"You heard me."

"You are *not* getting rid of my baby to keep your husband."

"Nolan, it's *my* body. I can do what I want with it."

"Over my dead body."

"That's exactly what you'll be if Dolan finds out."

"I don't care. I'm the father, and I have to have a say-so."

"I don't understand why we're going through this," I said as I crossed my arms over my chest. "All I wanted was to have a baby like any normal woman would." I started hyperventilating, crying, and trembling uncontrollably. Nolan called in a nurse to give me a shot, and I calmed down and fell asleep instantly.

Sometime in the middle of the night, I woke up worrying about my husband. The more I lay in that bed, the more I thought about what Chevette said about Dolan going out with that woman. Suddenly, the realization of what was happening hit me, and it just ate at me more and more, until, finally, I bolted out of bed, threw on some jeans, found my shoes, grabbed my coat off the coatrack, and snuck out of the rehab center dead set on getting my man!

Once I got to the street, I put up my thumb and hitchhiked a ride from an old man who was driving into town. He kept talking, and I didn't want to hear his chatter, but I nodded and smiled anyway. It was the least I could do since he was giving me a lift. When he turned on my street, I nearly broke my ass jumping out of the car, ran halfway down the block, and didn't stop until I saw my house. When I saw Dolan in the doorway, words couldn't express how happy I was . . . that was, until a woman pulled up.

"Who the hell are you?" I asked her. She looked at me like I was crazy, and I probably looked even crazier. My hair was all over my head, I had on a hospital gown with jeans pulled over it, and I looked like I just escaped from the insane asylum. I didn't care.

"Darica, what are you doing here?" Dolan yelled as he came out the door.

"Duh . . . I live here, and it looks like I'm just in time. I apparently stopped an early-morning booty call. The big question is, what is *this* bitch doing here?"

"She's a friend of mine. She just came to drop off some paperwork for me."

"She looks like she came to drop you off some pussy," I blurted out, even though I saw a yellow manila folder in her hand.

"Tonette, can you bring these papers over tomorrow?"

"I don't want this bitch coming to my house."

"The last time I checked, it was my house too, and you don't get to call the shots."

"Sure, Dolan," she said as she pretended I wasn't even there.

"Don't come back to this house. Meet him somewhere else."

"Fine," she said. "Sorry for the misunderstanding."

"You *should* be!" I yelled as she picked up her pace. Dolan grabbed me and pulled me into the house.

"Darica, why are you acting like this?"

"Because I want my man back."

"You should've thought of that before you checked out of the marriage."

"I didn't. I just had a moment of weakness. I want us to be like we were."

"We both know that's *not* happening." I got on my knees, looked up at Dolan, and started begging.

"Please don't leave me, baby. I'll do anything—anything you say."

"Darica, get up."

"I can't live without you, baby. I need you so much. I'll tell you anything you want me to."

"I have all the answers I need," he told me. "It's over between us." I watched Dolan walk away and slam the door to our home without looking back, and as far as I knew, he didn't care what happened to me.

I had no clothes, very little money, and I was too ashamed to go back to the rehab center or the home of friends or family, so I went to the garage until I could figure out what to do next. We never parked our cars there; it was more like a storage place than anything. The next thing I knew, there were flashing lights in front of our house, and I heard police sirens. I was pretty sure the staff at the center called Nolan and reported me missing.

"She's not here," I heard Dolan tell the police. "We had a fight earlier, and she left."

"Do you mind if we look around?" the officer said.

"Not at all."

I hid in a tiny closet in the back of the garage. There were a lot of empty two-liter bottles in front of it, so I didn't worry about being seen. The police flashed their lights briefly, but they didn't look very hard.

I waited until Dolan left later, then looked inside the house for food. After gnawing on a sandwich, I went into the guest room and lay down for a nap. I heard Dolan come home a few hours later and get on the phone. I stayed in the guest room unworried because I knew he wouldn't come in there. He talked to Tonette on the phone for about fifteen minutes while they planned to go out for a movie. He poured himself a drink, then went into our bedroom. I heard the shower running and eventually, the front door slam. I cried when I came out of the room and smelled his expensive cologne. He was going on about his life, and as far as I could see, he wasn't concerned about me at all.

After I watched him drive away, I grabbed some money from under the mattress, some clothes, and a few belongings, and packed them in a suitcase. It was about half past midnight when I was done. Dolan still hadn't returned, and there was no sign that he was even coming back home for the night, so I was pretty sure he was on a booty call, and I was a distant memory. I walked a few blocks to a donut shop where I bought a jelly-filled doughnut and a coffee, called a taxi, and waited for my ride. I had him take me to the other side of town where I rented a cheap hotel room. I thought about my life with Dolan and how it seemed to be so short-lived. I cried for several hours, never bothering to answer the many calls coming from my cell phone because I obviously had nothing to say to anyone.

A few hours later, I scanned the phone book for a clinic so I could terminate my pregnancy. I made the appointment and caught a bus there. I saw this lady with two kids on her lap and one in a stroller. She seemed to be doing a fine job in taking care of them. I smiled at the smallest girl. She was so cute with two little ponytails. I only wanted one child, and things had gotten so bad, I couldn't even handle that. I got off the bus feeling guilty about what I was getting ready to do. At the clinic were women of all shapes, sizes, and colors, from all walks of life. I sat down, filled out the forms, and wondered what their story was, then shook it off and prepared myself for the ordeal. A few minutes later, Nolan came in. I tried to use a magazine to hide my face, but he walked right over to me and yanked me out of my seat.

"What the hell do you think you're doing?"

"I told you this is my decision."

"Actually, it's not. They called to get clearance from your doctor, and I told them it was out of the question because you're too weak and unstable for the procedure. Let's go." I walked out of the clinic so embarrassed I wanted to crawl under a rock.

"I'm not going anywhere with you."

"Fine. I'll call a few friends and have you placed on a three-day hold."

"Go to hell, Nolan. You don't own me. You had no right to lie."

"I didn't lie. I don't feel your body can handle the abortion. It's your word against mine."

"I'll just leave here, have it done somewhere else, and start all over again in a new town."

"What the hell's the matter with you, Darica?"

"Just let me go. I have a bus to catch."

"Bus? What the hell?" I jerked away from him and tried to run, but I was no match for him. He grabbed me in a bear hug.

"Move. You did what you came here to do. I'm going home," I said as I sat at the bus stop heading east.

"Home is *that* way," he pointed.

"Not anymore. Dolan kicked me to the curb. I had to get a motel."

"In this part of town?"

"Yes. It's all I could afford."

"Oh, hell no. You're coming with me."

"No, thank you. I'll be fine."

"Darica, you don't know the first thing about living down here."

"I know more than you."

"That's it," he said as he grabbed me and threw me over his shoulder, kicking and hollering.

"Let me go. This is a kidnapping!"

"Shut up," he said as he threw me in the passenger seat of his Ferrari, fastened the seat belt, and dared me to move. Once he was behind the wheel, he headed in the opposite direction, and we rode in silence until we reached a suburb and a sprawling estate in the hills.

"Who lives here?" I asked.

"Us," he said.

Chapter Nine

Evette

"So, what does she want?" Carlena asked.

"Hell if I know."

"I know you know, bitch."

"Who are you calling a bitch?"

"You. Your sorry ass is probably why we're both sitting here."

"Go to hell. I know what I'm doing. I can get out of here before you can."

"I know what I'm doing too. I came up with the perfect plan to get my man back, and I was going to tell you about it, but fuck it now. You got me sitting up here, and this whore is about to kill us."

"All right, I'll come clean with you. I tried to kill her first. I tried to stab her in the back but, somehow, I messed up, and she got away."

"So, you mean to tell me we're here because you didn't complete the job? I told you that you were getting soft. I thought I taught you better than that. Looks like I'll have to play cleanup again."

"Neither of us got the job done, and if she kills us, we never will," I said.

"While you bitches are over there conspiring, let me give you something to cackle about. You tried to kill me," she said, pointing at me, "and this one over here got all kind of shit going on, including stabbing people in closets.

I should kill you *and* her just for *knowing* you, but since I know you got money, I'll let you make it if you pay me."

"How much do you want?" Carlena asked. I gave her the look of death.

"You never ask somebody how much they want. You try to negotiate with them, dumb ass."

"One hundred thousand from both of you," the hooker spat.

"I don't have it," Carlena said.

"Well, you shouldn't have opened your big mouth," I told her. "We don't carry around that kind of money."

"Just cut it. I'm not as stupid as I obviously look. I did my homework. Your daddy's worth millions, and he's got friends worth billions. All I want is a portion. Work it out, or I'll kill you right now."

"That won't be necessary," I told her. "I'll get you your money." I made a few phone calls, and within an hour, I had the money ready. "I need to go to the bank," I said.

"Sure, and I'm Boo Boo the Fool. You think I'm going to let you just waltz out of here?"

"How else are we going to get it?"

"Someone can leave it at a drop-off spot like they do in the movies."

"You're so lame," I told her. "It's not that easy."

"You need to make it happen," she said. "I don't have all day. My trigger finger is itching."

"Fine," I said. "Where do you want the pickup location to be?"

"Tell them to bring it to National Road and no funny business either."

"Okay," I said as I picked up my phone. After I made a couple of phone calls, we both looked at Carlena.

"What?" she said. "You didn't order enough money for me?"

"Hell no. You know I don't roll like that."

"If you loan me the money, I'll make it worth your while," she told me.

"What could you possibly do at this point?"

"I'll share my plan with you if you help me."

"Fuck your dumb-ass plan. I'll get enough for you too, but you better get my money back to me."

"I'll do that, and then some."

Carlena

As soon as the prostitute let us go, I made a beeline for the first car I saw and hitchhiked my way back to town. I had no money, and I looked like shit, but only one thing mattered to me—getting my man. I knew I had to pay, or one of them would spill the beans on what I did to Darica. That was one extra person that knew about it from Evette opening her loud mouth when she was talking to me on the phone. Sadly, the only person I could get money from was the very one I owed money to. I assaulted her door for dear life, and when she opened it up, she was mad as hell.

"What the hell are you doing at my house?" she spat.

"I'm sorry. Somebody held me hostage, and I had to negotiate my way out of it."

"How is that my problem?" she asked.

"How's my man doing?"

"I wouldn't know. I've been dodging his calls, and I was just about to cut him off cold turkey, when you're no-paying ass showed up."

"What? I paid you $50,000."

"That's only *half* my fee. I need the rest of it in order to finish him off. He's fine and knows how to lay the pipe and all, but he couldn't replace money if his brick were made of gold." I was a little upset at hearing her refer to my man's sexual prowess, but I let it go.

"About that . . . It's going to take a little longer than I thought to get your money. Actually, I need a loan."

"You have the nerve to ask for money when you *owe* me?"

"I wouldn't be asking if it wasn't an emergency. They are going to kill me," I lied.

"Then you need to be careful about the company you keep."

"Are you going to front me the money or what?"

"You better be glad we're family. I'll do it this time, but you'll be in my debt until you pay me back with interest."

"You got it, Cousin. What about Dolan?"

"I'm done with him. Since you can't pay me, there's nothing more I can do for you. Fortunately for you, I did enough for you to snatch him anyway from his wife."

"Thanks, Cuzzo," I said, smiling as I opened the door to leave.

My cousin Tonette was what I called a "Man Breaker," a woman that took a man away from his woman, broke him down, brought him up to her speed, got him ready to move on to another woman, and then dumped him. That way, it's easier for the next woman, usually the one that hired her, to step in and take over. In Dolan's case, she helped ease the pain and guilt of losing Darica, then left a huge void in his bed. It took me all of ten minutes to find out that Dolan and Darica were officially broken up, and then I moved in to grab my man.

Nolan

Dolan was the only thing Darica talked about. I couldn't lie. Hearing her pledge her undying love for him broke my heart. I hated watching her sulk, even more. But I had no reason to be upset with her. He was her husband of five years, and she'd known him for six. Although it was me who saved her that night, it was him she had a history with. I loved her with all my heart and soul, but I knew there was nothing I could really do about that. I let her vent, contemplating whether I should tell her that I was her hero, or if it would even make a difference at this point. I decided against it.

Darica didn't want to come live with me, but with her current situation, she didn't have much of a choice. Dolan was openly seeing other women and made it very clear he didn't want to be bothered. Being in the same household as him would only create more friction between them. The fact that she left the rehab center against medical advice didn't sit too well either. I convinced her and them that I was the only one capable of providing the type of care she needed outside of a medical facility, which she was dead set on not going back to. She didn't really have any other housing options.

Aside from all that, she loved the house. I gave her the master bedroom. It was large enough for her to put all her belongings in, plus a bassinet and crib for the baby. I figured I would eventually end up in there anyway. Dolan was on some straight dumb shit, and coming from a man who had been where he was trying to go, I figured it would be a long time before he came back from the head trip he was on. Having her in my house made me happier than a kid in a candy store.

Darica had a doctor's appointment and a meeting with her girls. She wasn't happy about it because she was about to come clean with them about the baby. It was about time. I planned to meet with my brother, Greg, and let him know what was going on before heading home to Darica, so we could somehow try to figure out a way to tell Dolan. He already knew she slept with somebody else—just didn't know who with. I was sure finding out it was me wouldn't soften the blow.

Darica

Nuni was the first to arrive. I was glad to have him in my corner because he was one of my biggest supporters. His instincts were right on point when I was in Nebraska, but I had denied it. I knew he wouldn't be happy that he was right about what went down between Nolan and me, but he wouldn't allow anyone to judge or berate me either. April came in next. She was already looking at me sideways, and I had a feeling she was on to me, for some reason. Finally, Chevette arrived. She was the least skeptical of the three and would accept me no matter what. I knew it seemed like a cop-out to start by telling them first, but Nolan and I had already decided we would meet with Dolan and tell him together, then deal with Rolanda, Mama C, and Millie later. I managed to avoid eye contact with all of them as we made our plates and enjoyed our food. I wanted to leave it at that and bask in the feeling of being with my friends once again. But, like all good things, that soon came to an end.

"So, why did you call us here?" Chevette asked me as soon as she scraped her plate clean.

"I called you here because I have something important to tell you."

"Spill the beans, girlfriend," Nuni said. April just looked at me and blinked. She knew it was going to be something crazy, so she tried to brace herself.

"I'm pregnant with Nolan's baby," I blurted. Nobody said anything. They just looked at me like I had a bad case of amnesia. All of them knew that I was undergoing treatment, and Nolan was my donor. There was a long, uncomfortable pause, so I took a deep breath.

"The treatments didn't work, so we did it the 'natural' way," I said. Everyone was speechless. Nuni put his hand on his chest like he was having a heart attack. Chevette's mouth flew wide open, and April closed her eyes and shook her head.

"What were you thinking?" April asked.

"I don't know. It happened so fast."

"Girlfriend, this is some crazy shit," said Nuni. "What are you going to do?" he asked.

"Are you having the baby?" Chevette asked.

"I'm not sure." They all looked at me like that was the stupidest thing in the world to say.

"Oh my God," April gasped.

"I tried getting rid of it, but Nolan wouldn't let me."

"Does Dolan know yet?" April asked.

"What did Dolan say?" Chevette prodded.

"He doesn't know. He knows the treatments didn't work, but not who I slept with."

"Shit," Nuni spat. "Don't worry, girlfriend. We stand with you. We'll get through this together."

"Thank you," I said as I grabbed his hand.

"You're not alone in this," April said. "I understand what you were going through. Nolan is slick, charming, and fine. That's a lethal combination. You saw how he had me going."

"So, you're not mad?"

"Of course not, sis. You're human."

"When are you going to tell your husband?" Chevette asked.

"Tonight. After Nolan gets back from telling Greg."

"Good. He should hear it from you."

"I don't know how to feel about this," April said.

"I don't think any of us do," Nuni said as he poured himself a drink from the bar.

"Liquor won't help me right now. I need chocolate," Chevette said.

"Give me the whole bottle," April said.

I spent the next couple of hours telling them, minus the graphics, about the events that occurred and exactly how everything went down. We talked, cried, and wiped each other's tears until we felt dehydrated. I was just about to see them out when I noticed my cell phone had accidentally dialed up Dolan. I hung it up at the same time a car pulled in the driveway. At first, I thought it was Nolan because the headlights blinded me. But when the man parked and got out, I could clearly see it was Dolan. He started running toward me, and I almost thought he was going to embrace me. The next thing I knew, his hands were around my neck, and he was choking me. I struggled to break free of him, but I was no match for his strength. I faintly heard Chevette beg him to let me go and saw April beating one of his arms. Even Nuni had trouble getting Dolan off me, but he gave a final shove and sent Dolan plummeting to the ground.

"What the hell is wrong with you, Dolan?" April asked.

"You know damn well what's up," he slurred. I smelled the liquor on his breath. "My wife just butt dialed me, and I listened to her confess she had sex with my brother."

"Fuck," Nuni sighed.

"Dolan, I was going to tell you. Did you hear *that* part while you were eavesdropping on my conversation?"

"No. I hung up as soon as I heard what you did."

"How did you know where to find me anyway?"

"GPS. I figured you were over here living with his low-life ass, and I was right."

"It's not like I had anywhere else to go. I couldn't depend on you, while you were over there digging Tonette out."

"Don't you dare make this about me! I tried getting back with you, but you insisted we break up. Don't worry about who I'm fucking. From now on, I'm living my life the way *I* want to live it. I'm *done* with you. I never want to see your cheating ass again."

"I can't believe you said that."

"I've never meant anything more in my life."

"Dolan, it's *not* what you think."

"The writing is on the wall. You lay up there and spread your legs for my brother to slide up in them. I'll never forgive you for that."

"Dolan, please. What about our baby?"

"You mean the bastard child of my brother's you're carrying? That's not *my* problem. I wouldn't want a baby with you to save my own life."

"You don't mean that."

"Keep living."

"Don't do this to me."

"Read my lips, Darica. We're *done*."

I couldn't say another word, couldn't chase him, or cry. All I could do was stand there and watch helplessly as my first love—my only love—walked out of my life.

Nolan

When I asked my brother Greg to come to Massey's, I was hoping he wouldn't be late. I was determined to get this off my chest so that I could get home to Darica, and we could break the news to Dolan. It was already seven o'clock, and there was no sign of Greg. So, I found a secluded table in the back, sat down, and watched the crowd.

I decided that I wouldn't order a drink until he arrived. God only knew how he would react, and I might need something stronger than scotch & soda. Soon, though, I heard a commotion, so I looked up. There was a crowd gathered around, and I heard yelling. I thought it was a bar fight . . . until I saw Greg and Dolan arguing. From the expression on Greg's face, I could tell Dolan was the angriest. Greg was pushing him toward the door, trying to keep him from coming into the bar, but Dolan was so mad, he was pulling Greg with him as he made his way toward me.

When they got close enough for me to understand, I knew what time it was.

"This low-life motherfucker fucked my wife. I'm going to kill his ass," I heard Dolan say.

I opened my mouth to say something back, but no words came out. The next thing I knew, he was punching me everywhere. I wanted to be the bigger one, so I didn't fight back . . . at first. I just grabbed him in a bear hug. He pushed my arms away like the Hulk. Instinct took over, and I started fighting back. The next thing I knew, we were in a full-blown fight, just like the one we had at Dad's house.

"Why, Nolan? Of all the people in the world, why did you have to fuck my wife?" he asked.

I was speechless. What could I say? I had done everything he accused me of, and there was no denying it. To top it all off, I had his wife living with me, and that had to be the stupidest move of all. I wished I could go back in time and not have done the things I did. I wished that their marriage would have worked out, and I hadn't asked her to come live with me. So many things I regretted came popping in my mind, but it was far too late now.

"We can work this out," I finally said. "We're brothers."

"You're no motherfucking brother of mine. I hate you, man. I hate you for me. I hate you for Darica. I hate you for being born. I hate you for every motherfucking thing you ever stood for. Not only are you not my brother, but you're also *dead* to me," Dolan said as he stormed out of the bar. Greg looked at me like he felt sorry for me, and so did some of the other bar patrons. The rest were horrified by what they heard. Either way, they were strangers to me, and I had no feelings about anything except for the pain of losing my brother over a woman I loved equally as much.

"Sorry, man," I said to Greg. "I was coming here to tell you tonight. Darica and I were going to break it to Dolan together, but somehow, he found out before we got a chance."

"I believe you," Greg said. "I just hope we can get through this and get back to normal again."

"Normal?" I said as I looked at him with a puzzled expression. "Does normal even exist in our family?"

"With a daddy like Brandon, probably not," he said as he shook his head. "But we've got to try."

I hugged the only brother I had left, then slinked out of the bar feeling like the scum of the earth, ran to my car, got in, and took the long, painful drive home to Darica. I felt the quicker I got to her, the quicker we could figure this out. When I got there, she was waiting at the door.

"I've been calling you," she said.

"I'm sorry I missed the calls. I was preoccupied."

She was about to say something when she saw my bruises. "What the hell happened to you?" she asked.

"Your husband happened to me."

"So, I guess he got to you too," she said.

"Too?"

"Yes, he came over here and choked the hell out of me."

"I'll kill him."

"No. I deserved it. We both deserved what we got. Now, we need to pick up the pieces and start over. I'm glad it's out there in the open. I lost my husband. That, I'm sure of. But I accept it."

She grabbed some gauzes and some bandages to clean my wounds. She was definitely no doctor, but whatever she did was making me feel better. Even though I was in pain, I still had what I wanted more than anything in life . . . Darica by my side. After she bandaged me, I got us a couple of glasses of water and asked her to sit down so I could tell her a story, the *real* story of what happened with Sheila, Ari, and the first day we met.

Chapter Ten

Darica

Six months later . . .

Nolan's story threw me for a loop. He had already told me how he had been in love with a woman named Sheila and how they had tried to conceive a child for months, but no matter what they did, she couldn't get pregnant. He told me how they had tried everything from seeing a specialist to considering adoption. He even mentioned that they had considered a surrogate, but up until now, he had never told me he actually found one. Now he was confessing what my friend Ari had already told me; that she had met a man who convinced her to carry a child for him and his fiancée, and they had made several failed attempts until finally, the two of them decided that they would have sex to get the child, and it worked. Nolan confirmed that he was the man Ari was speaking of. He told me she became obsessed with him and told Sheila that they had been having sex behind her back, and Sheila became so depressed that she took her own life.

If that wasn't enough, Nolan told me about the time he met me at the club and saved me from a man that tried to assault me. I thought he was Dolan the whole time because they looked so much alike, but in actuality, Dolan came to the parking lot after Nolan rescued me, while at the same time, Nolan was trying to find me. I married Dolan, thinking he was the man, he was my hero.

No matter which way you looked at it, I was floored. From finding out the truth about Sheila to finding out Ari was Nolan's ex-lover, to finding out Nolan saved me . . . It was all so surreal. I would never have pegged Ari for the girl Nolan chose to be their surrogate or the one that fell in love with him. How she played that off was beyond me. She had made several attempts to contact me, but I couldn't agree to meet up with her, and I was so glad I didn't. Friend or foe, I wasn't about to hang out with her anytime soon. All the women in Nolan's life seemed to be one can short of a six pack, and I damn sure didn't want to be caught in the crossfire.

As for Dolan, he really was done with me. Except for a few meet ups, he went on with his life just like he promised, bedding five or six women until finally settling on Carlena. I guess she got her man after all, and although it was up in the air whether they were lovers, it definitely looked like they were friends. There was nothing I could say or do. I'd made my bed, and we all know the rest.

I still lived with Nolan, much to the horror of everyone else. Rolanda was mad as hell when she found out everything, but she eventually got over the shock. She showed up unannounced with her road dogs, Millie and Mama C, and they gave us an earful.

"What the hell is the matter with you two? First, you fail to tell me you needed a donor; then you sexed each other like rabbits like it was in the do-it-yourself kit."

"What difference would it have made, Ma?"

"I could've helped you."

"Help with what, the turkey baster?" Nolan asked. Rolanda slapped the shit out of him, and he just took it. She then turned to me.

"What's *your* story?"

"I don't have one. I just let it get out of hand."

"What did we tell you about running? You should have told us what was going on."

"I wanted to, but I just didn't know how."

"You had other options, baby," Millie said.

"They made it sound so good; then when the treatments didn't work, I had a meltdown. I wish this weren't the truth, but it is. Can you forgive me?"

"We already have," Mama C said as the other women nodded. "You need to forgive yourself."

"How do I do that?" I asked more to myself than anyone else in the room.

"Only God knows," Millie said. "You said they made it sound good. Who are you talking about, the doctors?"

"The fertility clinic was Dolan's and my idea," Nolan said.

"Y'all do some crazy shit," Rolanda shook her head and said. "The child is here now. I'm going to make sure my grandchild has everything it needs."

"Thank you, Ma," Nolan said as he grabbed us all for a group hug.

I had to hand it to Rolanda. She was pretty open-minded if she could accept the mess I'd made and still be civil toward me. I guess, in the end, she decided that either way, she was going to be a grandmother, and I would be in her life. At least, two of her sons had given her a grandchild. Greg had finally taken a stand and asked Rella for a DNA test. If he were the father of her child, he wanted to step up to the plate to make sure the child actually benefited from the money he was providing.

Speaking of Dolan, he did take me to lunch one day and confided in me about what happened to him. Some doctor took it upon himself to make Dolan a guinea pig and gave him pills that messed with his fertility. Just the thought of all the trouble we went through had us crying like babies, but our lives had taken this turn, and we had to deal with it.

I never planned to be in this predicament, and I would never give up hope that my husband could be the father, but the scary part was the odds were against Dolan being my child's father, and the reality was that Nolan had most likely gotten me pregnant.

In addition to that, there seemed to be a paradigm shift. I knew Nolan would take care of the baby if it were his, but Dolan was now so messed up, I didn't know what he'd do or whether he'd leave me to raise the child by myself. Dolan was drinking like a fish. He said he was getting help for his problem, but somehow, I doubted that. At times, he was as irrational as all get-out, making it very clear that our lives would never be the same on the one hand and insinuated that we should still have sex on the other. One day, he would ask me to contact him if I wanted to discuss the baby and avoid me like the plague the next. He didn't seem happy about the possibility of the child being his at all. His temperament toward me was like night and day. Sometimes, I hardly even recognized him.

I talked to my doctor about the fact that my stomach was getting huge, so he scheduled me for a special clinic appointment. When he put the jelly on me and rolled the ultrasound wand, he discovered that I was pregnant with not one but *two* kids. I asked him to double-check because I had had an ultrasound when I got stabbed, and they didn't discover it. He laughed and said that often happens when one child is hiding behind the other if it's too early for the ultrasound to detect a child, or when they are concerned about focusing on something other than pregnancy. Now I was more scared than ever because I didn't know if I could raise two children on my own.

***

I was cleaning the big mirror in the front room while I waited for April to come over for lunch when a strange thought occurred to me. "What if I'd met Nolan first?" I looked at my reflection as I said those words out loud. I was trying to make excuses for it, trying to rationalize the unthinkable. Life definitely had no guarantees. "Even if I had met him instead of Dolan that fateful day, there was still no way of knowing what would have happened. Only God knows if he would've even loved me with the same intensity he does now. He may have dragged me through the mud, been immature, or still kept seeing those other women. Then where would I be? The man he was today was mature, had evolved, had renovated himself, and reconstructed every thought and deed he ever had in order to love me unconditionally, and I found myself loving him too."

"That's some intellectual shit." April clapped.

"How long have you been standing there?"

"Long enough to know Nolan whipped it on your ass good. You got it bad, girl. You better be glad Dolan didn't hear that."

"I'm thanking my lucky stars that he didn't. We've had enough problems with him to last us a lifetime."

"Dolan really has gone off the deep end, but I can't say that I blame him. If you were my wife, I would probably have done the same thing."

"Aaaaw, baby, I didn't know you cared," I teased.

"It's good to see you laughing. I know it can't be easy, with the rumors and all."

"You're right about that. It's funny how a good deed can turn into something totally opposite."

Although I was living with Nolan, our relationship wasn't sexual. We got pretty close and had a couple of run-ins a few times, but, ultimately, we decided we were best as friends. It took me several tries to get the point across that I wasn't feeling him like that, nor that I ever would. I was still stuck on my husband and fell into bed with him a handful of times until he finally got so wild, I couldn't handle it. Dolan played me like a fiddle and just like the song said, *"I'll be a fool for you,"* Dolan would call, and I would foolishly think he wanted to get back together and come running. As they say, fool me once, shame on you, fool me twice, shame on me. My ass kept coming back for more, letting him have his way with me until it finally came to a head with a grand finale that would make anyone wake up and smell the coffee.

"Is this what you want?" he yelled. He had convinced me to let him take me to lunch. All it took was a plate of food from Sea Breeze and our wedding CD, and I was in his bed.

"Yes, baby, yes."

"Tell me then."

"I want it, baby. Give me all of you."

"That's my girl," he said as he pumped me so hard, I had to grab the sheets. The CD was blasting, and Dolan was driving me crazy. He had my teeth clinching, and my toes curling. I had to blink twice to see if he was really my husband.

"I've never seen you make love so furiously."

"There's a lot you haven't seen me do."

"I love you, baby."

"Then why did you betray me?"

"I'm sorry, baby and it'll never happen again."

"Say it."

"I won't do it again."

"Lift your leg for daddy."

"Oh yes, baby," I said as I was coming. I suddenly saw something different in his face, and when I looked in his eyes, they weren't the same. They didn't hold my gaze like a man in love. It was more like a dog in heat. He carefully flipped me over on my tummy, then deeply rammed himself in me. I yelped in pain but found pleasure in the feeling. I cried out his name over and over, and he reached his hand around and stuffed a sheet in my mouth so that I couldn't cry out. I was apparently too loud for his taste. I thought it was strange, but I didn't care. My husband was back, and he had forgiven me for the unthinkable, was accepting me with open arms, and, damn, the sex was off the chain. I didn't know who or what he used to practice with, but whatever it was, it made him better.

"That's right, baby. Toot that ass up for daddy."

I came so many times, I lost count, and when he had his fill of me, he pulled out, jacked himself off, and came all over my behind. Now, *that* was a first. The sinister grin on his face told me that he wanted to say something, and it was not about to be good. Our lives had changed into something I didn't like. He must've thought better of it because he zipped up his pants, kissed me on the forehead, and got up. I waited for him to tell me to get my things and move back home, but the only thing he told me was to let myself out, and he would lock the door later. Somehow, he had reduced me to a number. I was no longer his Every, and he was nothing like the man I had affectionately called, My First Love. I walked out feeling defeated.

Nolan remained a true-blue friend to me. I think he knew that I was sneaking out to see my husband, but he never judged me. He just let me do me and had faith that I would realize how unproductive my marriage was.

Dolan hated the fact that I stopped jumping when he called, and I think he grew to resent me for it. Nolan seemed relieved that I stopped going wherever it was I was going and started spending more time with him.

He was inquisitive, wanting to know everything about me, everything I was feeling, and everything that no one else knew. He wanted to know what I was going through, where I grew up, and how it felt to have him growing inside me. Nolan took me seriously, and I loved that side of him just as much as the things that made me laugh. I didn't answer all his questions, but I definitely answered the last one.

"It feels like a fullness, happiness, and an overwhelming love. It feels like anticipation, anxiety, and an abundance of hope, like too much water and not enough food . . . a flood of emotions going through my body all at once."

"Can I ask you another question?" he asked.

"Shoot."

"What is the most extreme thing you ever thought about when it came to me?"

"I don't know what you mean. Maybe you should give me an example."

"Well, when I first saw how happy my brother was and found out it was you that he was marrying, I wanted to whisk you away and control you, put you in a little box, and be the only one that owned you. I wanted to send my brother on a trip to an island where he could have two or three of you because I knew I had the real, uncut, unadulterated, version."

"Wow. That's deep."

"In my heart, you were always mine. How about you?"

"Well, it looks like every woman you've been with has gone to the extreme."

"I'm only interested in you."

"The most extreme thing that comes to mind when it comes to you is how lucky I feel when I'm in your presence. You make me tingle and tremble, and I gush with excitement. I think about the life we would've had if you were my husband, how hard you love, and how deep you get. I think about the world within a world we could create together. The feelings seemed to have always been there, but they got stronger when you were saving my life on that operating table."

"Let me find out you low-key love me."

"Maybe next lifetime."

"Maybe in another country."

"Don't push it."

Dolan

Tonette turned out to be a real bitch. After we had sex, she barely wanted anything to do with me and wouldn't return any of my calls. I saw her out and about and confronted her about it.

"The least you can do is end it like a real woman and not like some kid."

"I don't owe you shit. I got what I came for, and it was good while it lasted."

"Really? Who are you working for?"

"Don't flatter yourself. Nobody asked me to do this. I was feeling you. You were a good lay, but it wasn't at all what I wanted."

"It's no sweat off my back. Your sex wasn't all that good anyway. You're a good-looking woman, but I'm already on to three other women who run circles around you."

"Good for you," she said as she wrestled her arm away from me and walked away. I knew she was on some bullshit, and it hurt my ego, but I wasn't going to chase after any woman, and after that run-in with Darica, I was determined that I would never commit to a woman or fall in love again.

Carlena showed up again after a long hiatus. I didn't ask her where she went, nor did I really care. As far as we were concerned, the only thing we could ever be was friends. She was helpful in some ways. She did a lot of the cooking and cleaning for me, even though I never asked her to, and once a week, we would have dinner together. I didn't want to fuck around with her because I didn't want her catching feelings again. I didn't have time for that in my life. She tried me time after time, but I never gave in. I was drinking a lot more, but it didn't stop me from redirecting her to the door. I knew letting her back in my life would turn out to be a bad idea, but I needed the company to keep from losing my mind. I felt that anything was better than nothing, and the void I was trying to fill could only be done if I weren't helpless and lonely. There were times when I wanted to beg Darica to come home, try to work it out, but I knew she wouldn't do it with all that I had going on. I sort of used the other women to keep me from backpedaling.

Miko and I were still hanging out. Carlena hated it. I think she felt threatened by the woman, but I wasn't feeling her like that. Miko was seeing the same man from six months ago, and she was pretty happy. I hadn't gotten a chance to go to therapy with her again, but she seemed to be making progress.

Darica was still heavy on my mind, no matter who or what I was doing. I knew she wanted everything to go back to the way it was, but I just couldn't do it. She had hurt me far more than I wanted to admit. The easiest thing to do was fuck her like I was inhuman, but the hardest was looking at how it made her feel. But she had allowed another man to violate her, and he wasn't just *any* man; he was my brother. I hated myself for the way we were, but there was nothing I could do about it now.

Carlena

I got Dolan back in a sense, but I didn't really have him back. Dolan, the straight-laced man I never thought would do anything drastic, turned into the biggest ho I ever met. He had three or four women he was involved with, sometimes two on any given night. That was okay because I knew eventually we would get back together.

Miko's ass started coming back around, and I hated it. I was uncomfortable because I felt she was trying to win Dolan over again, and I definitely didn't want her telling him about the setup years ago when he caught her with Nolan. I often wondered why she didn't tell him sooner, but I figured she was just too ashamed ever to want to revisit it. Besides, he had moved on from both of us and married someone else. There was no reason to dredge up old dirt.

Neither one of us could ignore the fact that Dolan was a far cry from the man he used to be. He had so many women, you couldn't even count them all on the one hand, and keeping up with them was a chore. Most of them knew their place. They knew not to come over unannounced and didn't dare overstep their bounds. Sometimes, people got bold, like the one that had the nerve to show up while we were having dinner one night.

As soon as we sat down to eat, we heard a loud pounding on the door.

"Open this damn door, Dolan," cried a female voice.

"What the hell," he said as he ascended the hallway and yanked open the sliding door. She had apparently climbed the fence and ended up in the side yard.

"What do you want?" he said to Ms. Fence Hopper.

"I've been calling you for a week."

"What do you want me to do about that?"

"You could at least call a sister and tell her you didn't want to be bothered."

"I'm sorry. I thought you got the picture ten unanswered calls ago."

"Don't be funny, Dolan. I see you're having dinner."

"Yes, and you weren't invited. So, if you will excuse me—"

"Hell no. I know you didn't just dismiss me. I'm trying to understand this new chick and why she's my replacement."

I wasn't going to say nothing to the basic bitch, but she took it there when she addressed me.

"First of all, I'm the chick he's been fucking since high school, and I'm still around. Don't be mad at me because you're a stank bitch who can't hold a man. Now, get out of my sight. I can smell you from across the room." I pinched my nose and squeezed my eyes shut like I was trying to endure her stench.

"You sorry bitch. Dolan doesn't want you."

"He cooked me dinner. I beg to differ."

Ms. Fence Hopper lunged at me like I was some girl in grade school, and I put my feet up and kicked her in the stomach. She let out a yelp as she landed on the floor. She looked like she wanted to get up for some more, but I lifted my fork and dared her to try. Dolan helped her up and escorted her to the front door.

"Don't come back," he warned her. That was when we decided it would be a good idea to meet over at my house more often.

One particular night, when I was in the mood, I invited him to dinner, and I was sure I had him, but he just turned me down and went home. I wanted him like nothing I've ever wanted in my life, but, unfortunately, that night I had to use my vibrator. It gave me a brilliant idea, however. Dolan was determined to be my friend. As a matter of fact, he prided himself on it. So, I used it to my advantage the next time I went over to his house.

"Dolan, can I ask you something from a male point of view?" I said.

"Sure."

"Well, I was wondering if a man can mess up a woman's insides."

"What do you mean?"

"Can his dick be so big that it could mess a woman up?"

"I don't think so," he said, looking confused. "I mean, a woman can bear a child, so I would think she could take a man of any size inside of her. Why do you ask?"

"I've been experiencing some discomfort with Carlos."

"Wow. Carlos is living large?"

"Yes. Carlos is packing," I said, almost choking on my water. There was an actual Carlos, but his ass not only missed the call for the well-endowed manhood line, but his dick was also smaller than my pinky finger. Having sex with him was like having no sex at all. I hated lying to Dolan, but, sometimes, you need to do drastic things to get drastic results.

"Maybe you should go to the doctor and get checked," he said as he loosened his tie. Got him. Nothing gets a man's goat better than the idea that another man, or even a vibrator, for that matter, was bigger than him.

"You really think so?" I asked him.

"Yes. The doctor is the best judge. Let him check it out and tell you what you need to do."

"Okay, I will, and thanks so much for the advice."

"No problem," he said.

I made a bed on the couch and immediately pretended like I was snoring. Dolan chuckled at me and went to bed like he normally did. This wasn't new. He was used to me getting the itis after dinner or drinking too much and passing out on his couch. We both had too much to drink, so I knew he was anxious to pass out. Sometime, in the middle of the night, I got in bed with him.

"Whoa," he said. "You know that's not cool. One of us has to sleep on the couch." He got up and wrapped a blanket around his naked bottom.

"Please, don't leave. I need your help. I need it bad."

"I'm sorry, Carlena. It's not that type of party."

"Why can't you make love to me?"

"What?"

"Why can't you pretend I'm just one of those other women?"

"Because they know their place. Besides, I don't want you like that."

"I asked you to do me one favor, and you can't even help me out. Are you that heartless?"

"Carlena, you have a man. You need to work things out with him."

"A man that's too big. I need a man that I can handle. I can't even enjoy sex with Carlos. Why can't we just get back together?"

"I don't want you or anybody. You know that."

"I love you."

Dolan looked at me like he felt sorry, but he made me leave anyway.

A few days later, I got a call from the owner of the bar a few blocks away. Dolan was there, and he had too much to drink. The bartender felt so bad that he started replacing water for the gin Dolan was ordering. I went to get him and helped him make his way to the car, into the house, and eventually to his bedroom. I started undressing him to put on his pajama bottoms when I noticed something standing at attention. I didn't know how it happened, but he was hard. I jumped on it with a quickness.

"Shit," he blurted and held up his hands to hold me off. "Fuck it," he eventually said. "Might as well." When I saw him give in, I was so ecstatic that I straddled him and went right to work. He didn't participate, but he let me make love to him the way I wanted to. I was in heaven. It didn't take long for us to reach a climax and collapse into sleep. After what seemed like a few minutes, I awoke to him pushing me off him.

"You want me to leave?"

"Yes. Lock the door on your way out."

"Why don't you want me to stay? That was amazing."

"You have to go," he said as he scowled at me.

"Why? Because I'm not your precious Darica?"

"For starters."

"Fuck you, Dolan."

"Get out, Carlena."

"I'm sorry. I had a moment of weakness, but it won't happen again. Can we still be friends?"

"Right now, I need you to go."

I left without a second thought. In fact, the only thought I had when Dolan kicked me out was squeezing my legs together and carefully waddling to the car. Once I got in, I scooted down as far as I could to the edge of the seat, tooted my pelvis up, clinched my PC muscles, and lifted my left leg, so that I could keep the sperm in my body. Once I arrived home, I walked in my house the same way and immediately plopped on the couch. I was planning to lie upside down for at least twenty-four hours.

Dolan talked a good game, but when I looked into his eyes, I saw how horrified he was. I knew when I caught him off guard, it was too early, and he was too drunk to be rational. He wasn't prepared for the way I pounced on him. Right about now, he was thinking about how he not only had sex with me but came inside me as well. It was no secret now that he was capable of getting a woman pregnant, and I knew the thought of having a baby with me scared him shitless. He had to be mad as hell for slipping up. For his sake, he better hope and pray that none of his seed got far enough inside of me to hit any of my eggs, because if I were pregnant by him, I was going to give new meaning to the words, *"Run with it."*

Chapter Eleven

Nolan

It took a few months, but Evette found out where I lived. How she found out, I didn't know, but I was determined that she was never going to step foot in our house.

"I don't know why you thought you could keep me away by running, but what you had to know was that I wasn't going to stay away for long."

"What do I look like running from you? You're nothing to be scared of."

"I can't believe you had the nerve to bring that bitch to live with you like it's a fairy-tale love affair or something," she said, ignoring me. "Darica has to be the luckiest bitch in the world because clearly, nobody is angry at her for sleeping with you. I guess her husband is used to sharing women with you."

"Go straight to hell, Evette. I don't give a fuck what you think."

"To top it all off, you got the place all decorated to appease her, like y'all are an item or something," she said as she pushed her way into our house like she was running shit. I grabbed her arm and pulled her right back out like she was contaminating it.

"Time for you to go," I said. She looked hurt and angry as she scowled at me, yanked her arm away, and walked off like she was going to pay me back somehow.

As soon as she sped off, Mina called. I was happy to see
she was okay, but I didn't think it was cool for her to contact me. I was done with her, just about as done as I was
with Evette. I was cordial to Evette because I loved her father, and, to me, he was the best thing since sliced bread,
but what I wasn't going to do was tolerate anyone who
hated so much that I had with me the person that I wanted more than life itself. My mother was so outdone about
Darica being pregnant that she had barely got around to
telling me how Evette snuck on her property. I saw Mina
calling and was going to ignore it, but she had been nothing but good to me, even though I didn't want her. So, I
decided to take the call this time.

"Hello," I answered.

"Thank you," she said.

"For what?" I asked.

"For answering the phone. I've been trying to get in
touch with you forever."

"Mina, I thought I told you I didn't want anything to do
with you."

"You did, and I understand how you feel, and I moved
on with my life. I'm just trying to help."

"With what?"

"You're in danger. At least, the people around you are."

"What do you mean?"

"I'm so sorry. I should have come to you a long time ago,
but I was scared, confused, and broke."

"What are you talking about?"

"Evette came to me and threatened me. When I told her
I didn't care about my life, she offered me money to send
me far away from you. What she didn't know is I wasn't
the real threat, the one taking your heart."

"I don't understand where all this is coming from."

"Understand this. Darica is in a lot of danger. You need
to keep her as far away from your ex as you can. Evette is
insane."

"I'll keep that in mind, and thank you for the call."

"You're welcome. I wish you the best in your life."

"Thanks. Same to you."

I hung up the phone, trying to understand where Mina was coming from. Evette had a temper, but I never thought of her as dangerous. I would never think she would hurt anyone. She always seemed so upscale. Now, she was over-the-top crazy for me, but was she sick enough to cause bodily harm? I had pretty much charged it off to some sort of crazy trip Mina was on until Darica decided to go to a doctor's appointment by herself. I begged her to take me, but she wanted to remain independent. I think she was a little ashamed of me and didn't want to be seen with her "baby daddy" in public, especially after her coworkers started tripping at her job.

Darica

Against my better judgment, I started back working. Being seven-and-a-half months pregnant with twins was no walk in the park, and I was so big that I could barely drive. But I wanted to be doing something other than sitting around the house all day. It was enough I was labeled as Nolan's new lover. I didn't want to be labeled as a gold digger as well.

Everything seemed to be going okay. I fell right back into place teaching art to kindergarteners. It didn't occur to me that something crazy would happen. Aside from Carlena, I didn't think anyone had any ill intent toward me, and even that was a result of her being threatened by my marriage to Dolan. Now that she had him where she wanted him, I had no reason to fear for my safety. I wasn't really anticipating anything crazy happening.

One morning, I got to class and was surprised that none of my students were there. I was always punctual and tried to instill the same ethic in them and some of their parents. I was early and made sure I had my lesson plans for my students. The next thing I knew, the principal came into my room and asked me to come to his office.

"What about my class?" I said.

"I've made arrangements for your class. It'll only take a minute."

"Sure," I said, thinking nothing of it. I hoped that everything was okay with his family, the school, the parents, the students, and the other teachers as I made my way there.

"Please have a seat," he said.

"I'd rather stand. What's this all about?"

"Well, it seems as if some of the students are talking about you being an unwed mother."

"I'm still married."

"Well, that's the problem. You have a husband, and you're living with your lover. Some of the parents think that's a negative image to portray to their kids."

"I'm actually staying with my brother-in-law until my husband and I work out our differences. What do the kids know about all that?" I asked.

"One of the children came up to one of the teachers and said, 'Miss Rogiers is having an affair.' I don't know if this child has any idea what an affair is, but the fact that she was able to repeat it speaks volumes. I'm going to have to ask you to go on a leave of absence until we can investigate this."

"What? I can't believe this. This is my job we're talking about. What I do behind closed doors is my business. I'm a good teacher."

"I understand that, and we'll do everything we can to bring you back as quickly as possible, but we have to do what's best for the children. I'm sorry, Miss Rogiers, but

I'm going to have to ask you to take all of your personal belongings with you for now. We'll be in touch."

I was horrified. I never thought that I would potentially lose my job over getting pregnant. I was too devastated to call anybody, so I simply left the school and headed for my doctor's appointment.

My blood pressure was a little high, and my obstetrician told me to take it easy, but he confirmed that everything was okay with the babies, and I headed back home. Nolan wanted to come and meet me for lunch, but I decided against it. I should have called him back as soon as I saw that I had a flat tire, but I decided to call the towing company instead.

After I made the call, I sat on a bench in front of the doctor's office and grabbed a book to read. About ten pages into it, I heard some girls fighting in the background. The next thing I knew, they were dangerously close to my bench. I tried to move and get out of their way, but whenever I would move over, they moved over with me.

One of them threw me down on the ground, and another started kicking me; then another started punching me in my head and face. I still had my purse in one hand and my keys in the other when I remembered I had pepper spray attached to my key chain. It was kind of old, and I wondered if it even worked, but I had to try something. I sprayed it, their punches slowed down, and they eventually ran. I was able to run back into the doctor's office and call the police. I thought about calling Dolan, but I was pretty sure, at this point, he didn't care about me, so I called Nolan.

"Hello."

"Nolan, I need you."

"What's going on?"

"I'm at the doctor's office. Something happened."

"I'm on my way. Stay on the phone and talk to me."

"Some girls attacked me. At first, I thought it was just a girl fight that I was too close to, but when I tried to move away, they started hitting me instead."

"What?"

"Nolan, I'm scared."

"I'm not too far away. I'll be there in five minutes. Are you safe?"

"Yes. I'm inside the doctor's office, and the police are here. Hurry."

"I'm just about there."

When Nolan arrived, he immediately grabbed and embraced me, looked at my bruises, and asked, "Do you need to go to the hospital?"

"No. They already asked me that, and I told them no because I'm pretty sure my doctor can handle it. He can check on the baby as well."

"That's a great idea," Nolan said.

"I examined them and determined that everything is okay, but I want to run some tests just to make sure that the babies aren't in trauma," my doctor said. That was how Nolan found out I was having twins.

"Babies? When were you going to tell me?" he asked, smiling from ear to ear.

"I was going to tell you once I had more time to process it myself."

"Okay, but I wish you would stop keeping things from me. I'm the father, and I want the best for you and my kids."

"I understand. I'll do better."

"Thanks," he said with a sigh of relief. "I wasn't going to say anything, but Mina called me with a prediction, warning, or whatever you want to call it, and it's starting to ring true. She was trying to help me, and for that, I'll always be grateful. But what I can't understand is how and why she knew something bad was going to happen."

"Do you think she's sincere about it?"

"She's definitely on point. I need to find out if Evette had a hand in this, and there's only one way I'm going to find it out. I'm paying her a visit. I have to see the whites of her eyes."

"Be careful, Nolan."

"I will."

Nolan took me to April's house, and what did he do that for? My bestie went completely berserk.

"What the fuck?" she said when she saw my bruises. "Tell me who the hell did this so that I can kick their ass."

"I wish I knew, sis, but I'm going to find out," I said.

"I'm about tired of these bitches," she reiterated. "Let me find out who's doing this shit, and I promise you they got an ass whipping with my name on it."

"Calm down, sis," I said. "We'll get to the bottom of this sooner or later."

Evette

When Nolan approached me, I thought I had died and gone to heaven. I took in the smell of his heavenly cologne, and my eyes traveled from his face to his chest to the perfect bulge in his pants. I wanted him so badly that my mouth started to water. I had prayed that one day he would come back to me, but when he started questioning me, it was an entirely different spiel than what I had imagined. Instead of pledging his undying love and inability to live without me, he started spewing some mess about Darica's attack. I should have known his lovesick ass was only coming to ask me something about her.

"I think you know why I'm here."

"I don't see a ring in your hand, so I'm assuming it's not to ask me to marry you."

"Quit playing, Evette. Darica was attacked," he ignored my words and said.

"So, what do you want me to do about it, call the police?"

"Don't be sarcastic. I came to ask if you had anything to do with it."

"Hell no. I'm not thinking about that simple bitch."

"Only that she's a simple bitch."

"Why are you wasting your time with her, Nolan? We could be so happy together."

"You know as well as I do, you're *not* the woman for me."

"I would do anything for you. Doesn't that count?"

"I don't love you, Evette."

"You used to. Think about our baby."

"Yeah, right. If you find out anything about the attack, let me know."

He left just as quickly as he arrived, leaving me to smell his erotic cologne and my heart in shambles. I had a temper tantrum right then and there, throwing glasses and breaking up anything within reach and in my sight.

"I hate this, and I fucking hate Darica. She's got Nolan coming over here threatening me and shit. She's worse than that bitch, Sheila. I should push her off a building too."

My phone rang, and when I looked down to see who it was, I saw that it was my daddy. He wanted to know when he could meet me, and I told him right away. I straightened up my place and got ready for his arrival when I noticed something was amiss. A television was on in a back room that I knew I hadn't left on. I walked in and saw Payne sitting in the La-Z-Boy watching TV.

"Hey, honey. How was your day?"

"I'm not your honey, and what the hell are you doing here? Didn't I tell you to get lost? What are you, homeless or something?"

"I was just checking on you, love. I've been worried about you lately," he whispered, ignoring all three questions.

"I'm fine."

"That you are, but you've been sick, and I want to make you feel better."

"I'm not in the mood for that right now. Besides, Daddy's on his way over."

"It's cool. I can wait."

"The hell you can. Get the fuck out of my house."

"That's no way to talk to your future husband."

"You really are delusional if you think I'm marrying you." Payne didn't say anything. He just smirked and got on his phone to pull up some information. Suddenly, I heard my voice and saw my image on his screen. He was replaying footage of me having the outburst a few minutes ago. I tried to wrestle the phone away from him, but his grip was tight as hell. I knew if he showed it to anyone, I would be doing some serious time for Sheila's murder.

"What do you want?"

"I think you know that," he said as he pulled out a diamond ring. We heard a knock at my door, and Payne got up and went toward it.

"I'll get that," he said. "It's probably your dad."

As soon as Daddy walked in, he had a look of concern. "Why did you call me and ask me to arrange to meet my daughter here?" he asked Payne.

"I have something very important to tell you," Payne said.

"Is it urgent?"

"That depends on what her answer is."

"I don't understand. Why do you need me here just to ask Evette something?"

"I wouldn't dream of asking her to marry me without asking you for her hand. Evette," he said as he kneeled, got on one knee, and pulled out the ring once again, "will you be my wife?"

My eyes got big as saucers because I knew if I said the wrong thing, Payne would rat me out, and I would lose my daddy, my freedom, and, ultimately, Nolan.

"Yes," I said as I gave him a death stare, then forced a fake grin as well. Daddy and Payne hugged and congratulated each other, but I was mad and sick. I ran to the bathroom to throw up my lunch.

Darica

Nuni, Chevette, and April did everything in their power to make me feel better, but it was no use. I'd always hated the holidays, and now was no different. It was getting dangerously close to Christmas, and, as always, I didn't feel all the effort people put into the holiday was worth it. If I thought I was depressed before, I really had something to be sad about now. I had no job, was living with a man everyone thought was my lover because I had sex with him one time, and I couldn't go anywhere by myself because someone was out to get me.

Since the house was so big, Nolan brought huge vases and paintings in an attempt to fill it up. I wasn't impressed. I didn't want to be a part of anything that remotely reminded me of happier times with Dolan since he, and only he, signified happiness. My husband wasn't dealing with any part of me, let alone spending time worrying about me, so I felt that any event was a wash, and it didn't mean a thing. Nolan bought so many gifts that I thought he had lost his mind. He placed them on my bed so enthusiastically; it was like we were man and wife instead of the deadbeat couple folks pegged us to be. Everyone of importance seemed to have cast us out because, in their mind, we plotted the affair from the jump. I couldn't help but wish I had followed my first mind and not allowed my husband and his fly-by-night brother to talk me into anything.

On the brighter side of things, the twins were coming along nicely, and I was enjoying the sensations, pampering, and attention that went along with motherhood. The babies kicked me so much that I thought I was a human football field. I marveled at the two lives that were living inside me and wondered how God could create such a complicated thing.

Another month had passed, and I reluctantly went to my doctor's appointment with Nolan. Despite the fact we hadn't had a paternity test, he acted out the role of a proud father who wouldn't let anyone steal his moment, no matter what. I hated going to the appointments because all they did was make me drink a whole bunch of water, weigh me, and tell me to stop eating salt. Anyone that knew me knew I loved to eat junk food. I had so many Snickers, Hostess CupCakes, ice cream containers, packages of frozen fries, and different kinds of soda in the house that you would have thought I was opening my own grocery store. Sugar and salt were the only things that made me feel better.

We arrived at the doctor's appointment early and sat down and waited to be called. Nolan wanted to hold my hand, but I wrestled it away from him. I didn't want anyone to associate us as a loving couple because that was something that we definitely were not. I started squirming in my seat because we had waited so long, my behind felt like it had cement in it. I was ready to call it quits and tell Nolan we should reschedule when Carlena walked in. She didn't look to be pregnant, so I thought she was coming in for a gynecology appointment. Boy, did she shock me when she went to the receptionist desk and started talking.

"Hi, I'm here to see a doctor. I'm pregnant!" she shouted.

"Can you lower your voice?" the woman at the desk told her. "I can hear you fine. Fill this out, and we'll be with you momentarily."

"OK. My man and I are so happy. This is our first baby," she volunteered.

"That's great, but I need you to fill out the paperwork so we can get you started."

"Will this take long?" she asked, looking behind her to stare at me.

"It shouldn't take too long once you start writing," the receptionist said.

"Fine," she said as she grabbed the clipboard.

I didn't think anything of it, except for the fact that I wondered who the hell got this bitch pregnant. When she picked up her phone and started dialing someone, I got my answer.

"Dolan," she said as loud as all get-out. "You need to answer this phone because I don't appreciate having to come to this doctor's appointment alone. I didn't make this baby by myself."

I was horrified, and my heart was beyond broken. I wanted to cry, but I didn't want her to see me sweat, so I just had to grin and bear it. If Dolan had unprotected sex with Carlena and got the lousy whore pregnant, it was his business. We were all adults and getting divorced was next on our to-do list anyway. I was a little hurt that he chose her to bear his firstborn child, but I was sure he felt the same way about Nolan. Nolan looked at me in disbe-lief, and I hunched my shoulders.

"I guess you're going to be an uncle," I told him.

Nolan

The detective that interrogated me ended up being the same one that came over to investigate Darica's attack. He looked like hell frozen over with grungy jeans, a matching T-shirt, and a suitcoat. I mean, who picked this lame's wardrobe? As usual, he was wielding dragon breath. I decided to do most of the talking to spare Darica the trouble.

"As you can see, my sister-in-law is pregnant and, unfortunately, not feeling well. I can tell you anything you need to know."

"She'll have to be the one to give the statements," he said, looking at me suspiciously. I prayed he wouldn't make another comment about us being close.

"I can do it," Darica said as she nodded her head that all was fine.

"Mrs. Rogiers, this is your second attack in six months. Is there anything you want to tell me?"

"Like what?" she asked.

"I have to tell you, I've never seen one person get brutally attacked so many times without some kind of history of abuse or foul play."

"Are you saying she asked for this?" I asked him.

"No. I'm simply saying these can't be isolated events. She must know the attackers or is being targeted by someone who does."

"I was innocently sitting on a bench after a doctor's appointment!" Darica shouted in protest.

"Yes. But the first attack happened in your very own mother-in-law's house. That was a pretty bold move. I won't press you about it now, but if you think of any reason why someone would want to hurt you like this, please call me."

"I will."

"Fine. I'll let you get back to whatever it was you were doing," he answered sarcastically.

Darica looked exhausted and was just about ready to lie down for a nap when we got a knock on the door. She decided to answer it and was immediately served with divorce papers. She quietly laid them on the coffee table and grabbed the keys to her car. I wanted to protest, but I understood that some things had to be done on your own.

"Make sure you have your phone so you can call if you need me," I told her.

"I have it right here," she said as she eagerly walked out the door.

Darica

The wind was torturous as it whipped through my hair and around my neck. I fastened my coat tighter around me and made the humiliating trek to my car. In a span of a few months, I had lost my husband, family, and dignity. Those divorce papers sent a message that my life as I knew it was officially over. I knew Dolan wasn't home, as he always spent Saturday mornings playing basketball with Greg, so I took the opportunity to grab some more of my things from the house. I could see from the corner that Dolan hadn't bothered to take care of the lawn. My garden was another story. The house stood out from the others on the block, not only because it didn't have a freshly manicured lawn, but the grass was brown and unruly throughout the yard.

I saw Dolan's car there and almost made a U-turn and headed back in the direction I came from when I saw the bright red "For Sale" sign. I immediately stopped the car and got out, so I could view the realtor's information and take down the phone number. I couldn't help myself. I knocked on the door.

"What do you want?" Dolan asked. I hardly recognized him with the beard he had grown since the last time I saw him, and I could smell the liquor on his breath.

"I want to know why you're selling my house."

"*Your* house?" He laughed. "Last time I checked, it was mine. You told me adding your name wasn't important." He was right. When we got married, Dolan had already started the process of buying the house, and I foolishly signed away my rights, thinking it didn't matter. In fact, last year, when I was renovating it, I purchased everything as a contractor and had Dolan sign off on the work as if it were a business transaction. I loved that house. My blood, sweat, and tears were in it, and the thought of losing it made my heart ache.

"You can't do that," I cried.

"I can, and I will."

"You are so evil."

"You fucked my brother, and *I'm* the evil one? He bought you a minimansion. What do you want with this house?" I took one look at my soon-to-be-ex-husband and knew he was only doing this to be spiteful.

"Nolan and I are not together."

"You could've fooled me."

"I can't believe you're so ignorant."

"Whatever. I'll stop the sale if you make it worth my while."

"Fuck you, Dolan," I spat.

"Ain't nothing here but space and opportunity," he said as he opened the door wider, as if to say, "Come on in and handle that."

But I just took one last look at the monster I created, rolled my eyes at him, walked back to my car, and sped off.

Nolan

"You bitches are going to get cursed out," April told Chevette and Nuni. "Darica hates surprises."

"She only hates it because of the birthday curse. Nobody said anything about a baby shower omen," Chevette said.

"Careful, Darica wouldn't choose yellow for her theme."

"You're just mad because yellow is your favorite color, and you don't want nobody to steal your shine," Nuni said.

"I'm telling you, she's not going to be happy with any of this. Tell them, Nolan."

"I know one thing. If Darica's going off on anybody, it damn sure ain't gon' be me," I told them, then looked at Nuni. "Maybe you should have it at your place."

"I live at the Sheraton," he said.

"Don't look at me," Chevette said. "I live with Ro."

"My place is being renovated," April said, "but even if it weren't, I don't want no part of this. Let's just tell her, so she can help us plan it."

"You're no fun," Nuni chuckled.

"Just tell me what?" Darica asked when she walked in.

"About the New Year's Eve party we're planning," Chevette lied.

"My big butt is not participating in no New Year's party," Darica told them. "What are y'all doing here anyway?" she asked.

"We came to see you. You been antisocial lately, and we wanted to catch up," Chevette said.

"If that's not the pot calling the kettle black, I don't know what is. Your stuck-up ass acts like you don't know nobody since you got with Gregg with two *g*'s," Darica said.

"Stuck-up? I always reach out to you. *You're* the one who's never free."

"That's because I'm not interested in taking my fatness to no club."

"You are the tightest pregnant chick I ever seen. You just want to sit around and talk like some old lady," Nuni said.

"Hello? It's not like I can walk up in the club and get my boogie on. We're all here now, so let's play catch-up," Darica said.

That was my cue to leave. I did not want to hear them cackle about men, vaginas, and whatever else divas talked about, and I knew they damn sure didn't want me there.

Darica

I was glad when Nolan left the room because I was sure Nuni was going to slip up and say something crazy, and I was so right.

"Is it true what they say about pregnant women?" he asked.

"What?"

"I heard they get real horny and want to pounce on their men."

"I wouldn't know."

"You mean you ain't banging the hell out of Nolan?"

"Nuni!" Chevette said while looking around to make sure the man in question wasn't in earshot.

"Eeeeew. Hell no. I told y'all the only interest I ever had in Nolan was as a friend. After he and I did that 'business transaction,' and I got what I wanted, we went right back to our original state."

"Business transaction?" Chevette asked.

"Original state?" Nuni screamed.

"Well, damn," April said. "Sounds like you got it all figured out. Too bad nobody told *him*."

"Girlfriend, he has it bad for you. If those hormones start acting up, you won't be able to control yourself. I would stay on his good side, so he can give you what you need," Nuni said.

"Hell yeah," April said as she gave him a high five. "Don't look at me, bestie. I'm over him. I haven't looked at him twice since I found out about you two, but you better get that."

"That's all fine and good, but I have a husband."

"Girl, Dolan is gone. He's so far over the deep end; it's like he's somebody else."

"You got that right," I admitted. "The day I found out he put the house up for sale, he treated me like shit. I hardly even recognized him."

"Put the house up for sale? He can't do that. You guys are going through a divorce. That's your house too."

"Actually, he owned it before we got married. I gave up my rights to the house."

"But you love that house. You worked your ass off renovating it."

"Yes, but I guess I'm just going to have to get over it. Either that or have sex with Dolan."

"What?"

"Yes, he propositioned me. He told me that if I fuck him, he'll let me have the house."

"That's brand new. I think Dolan is just yanking your chain. He can't be that cold."

"I'm going to be honest with you. At first, I was in a whole lot of pain, and I wasn't even thinking about sex, but after my body healed and the pain went away, I felt like jumping Dolan, Nolan, *and* a few vibrators."

"Nasty bitch!" Nuni screamed. "You gave him some, didn't you?" Everybody laughed.

"A couple of times."

"We've all been guilty of having sex after a breakup."

"I honestly don't want Dolan like that. With him, it's all or nothing. I really wanted my marriage to work. I know he's fooling around with other women, but I can't help but hold on to the dream that one day we'll be back together again."

"I feel you," Chevette said. "For a long time, I held the hope that Greg and I would be OK, but now, I'm over it."

"I'm done with pretty boys," April announced.

"What did you do, April?" Chevette inquired.

"I finally gave Grant a chance. I've been seeing him for a while, and everything is working out."

"You didn't tell your bestie?"

"Sis, I wanted to wait until I felt comfortable enough to announce it. Everyone had their own issues, and I didn't want to bombard you all with my antics. I'm having a wonderful time. We're taking it slow. I haven't slept with him, and he's taking me to dinner at his mother's."

"Wait a minute, bitch," Nuni said as he held his chest. "You kept your legs closed for a change, and you *still* get to meet the mom?"

"I already knew her. I told you we grew up together."

"That's so cool. I remember you talking about him from time to time. I always knew you had a crush on him. What changed?" I asked.

"I changed. I used to think of him as boring until I found out he was exactly what I needed."

"I'm happy for you, sis."

"It's long overdue," Chevette agreed.

"Now, you can stop being a slut," Nuni joked.

"Shut up, Nuni. You've been quiet lately. What do *you* have going on?"

"I've settled down myself. Got me a fine man I met at school."

"School?" we all screamed in unison.

"Yes. A bitch can't get edumacated?"

"What about your house and job and Nebraska?"

"That's gonna have to wait. I think I found the love of my life."

"I ain't even mad," April said.

"I'm happy for you all," I smiled.

"What about you, Darica? What will you do?"

"Well, after I drop these babies, I'm going to pursue my interior decorating business."

"It's messed up that you got suspended from your job."

"They offered it back to me. But I refused, got me a lawyer, and I'm going to see about suing them."

"Good for you," Nuni said. "But what about your marriage?"

"Like you said, my marriage is over. I may as well move forward. Who knows, maybe God will send me a good man eventually. But it's no rush. I'm cool for now."

"Amen. I'm sure He will."

"But I know what isn't cool."

"What?" they all asked.

"When bitches try to give me a surprise baby shower with a yellow theme."

Everybody cried in laughter. "How did you know?" Nuni asked.

"You have a big mouth." I laughed. "Besides, you know I like it when we all plan stuff together."

"Then that's exactly what we'll do," Chevette said. "Sorry, chica. We should have listened to April."

"Of course," April agreed. "I'm *always* right."

We all noshed on leftovers from the dinner that Nolan made the night before; then I walked my friends out and went to lie down for a long overdue nap.

Chapter Twelve

Darica

Nolan surprised the hell out of me. I wasn't doing much of anything lately, and he picked up on it and decided he was going to take me out to dinner. Not just any dinner but dinner at Chez Mizelle. I loved the restaurant, even though I had only eaten there once. Back then, I couldn't even afford a whole dinner. It was more like an appetizer. He'd bought me a silver Versace evening gown and placed it on my bed while I was in the shower. He did a wonderful job picking it out, and the size was perfect. I thought that was a miracle in itself because my big ass could barely fit anything.

I had to admit . . . He was a force to be reckoned with in his tux. That was the main attire for most of the men at the restaurant. When we got there, they took my coat and escorted us to a secluded table away from everyone in the VIP section, and many of the customers envied us.

"Order anything you want on the menu," Nolan said.

"Nolan, this is too much."

"No, it's not. You deserve it and much more."

"I hope you don't think this is a date because we are friends."

"I understand." He nodded. When I opened the menu, I almost screamed. Everything was over $300.

"My God. I can't afford this."

"It's on me. I invited you to dinner, remember?"

"I can't let you do this. I should pay half."

"I won't let you. Just enjoy your dinner."

"I don't know what to choose," I said.

"Let me help you," he said as he made several choices off the menu and told the waiter to bring it out quickly.

"Good choices, sir," the waiter responded.

About halfway through dinner, Dolan walked in, and I couldn't believe my eyes. He didn't have on a tuxedo but a very flashy outfit that I would never have thought I would see him in. On each arm, he had a bad bitch, and each was dressed to the nines. I almost thought he had given up his day job and started pimping instead. Don't get me wrong. It was all in good taste. It just would've been worn best by Nolan.

He didn't see me at first because of the location we were at. We could clearly see everyone who came and went out of the restaurant, but the only way anyone could see us was if someone spotlighted our tiny section.

I felt sick to my stomach, wondering what Dolan planned to do with the women he was sporting. I found myself thinking about him a lot lately and didn't know why I did this to myself because he was obviously enjoying his life. I, on the other hand, was feeling guilty about being on this little outing tonight. I guess a part of me wanted to punish myself for my deeds of the past.

I wanted to alert Nolan, but he was so engrossed in pleasing me, he noticed little that was going on around him. Besides, I didn't want to ruin his evening. We were almost finished and ready to go when Nolan decided to have a slew of exotic desserts sent to our table. They looked so exquisite that people started pointing at the flashy, unique creations, and we were the awe and envy of the customers. As soon as the special VIP Spotlight shined on us, I looked up—and straight into the eyes of Dolan. He wasted no time coming to our table to harass us.

"Well, if it isn't my wife and brother on a date!" Dolan yelled. Nolan gritted his teeth and shook his head. "Hello, wifey. You look stunning. I don't think I ever got a chance to congratulate you on your bundle of joy—I mean twins. I almost forgot my brother popped not one but two babies in you."

I closed my eyes and shook my head as tears fell freely from my eyes.

"Oh, don't be ashamed now. You weren't crying when he was banging your back out."

"Dolan, that's enough. Darica already feels bad enough. You don't have to humiliate her."

"Humiliate? You don't know the meaning of the word. Your wife didn't cheat on you. Oh, I forgot, you don't have a wife. Your bitch jumped off a building, so she wouldn't have to tolerate your cheating ass, so you decided to take mine."

"Is everything okay?" our waiter nervously asked.

"Yes. We were just leaving," Nolan told him as he dropped twenty one hundred-dollar bills on the table. "I hope this will cover everything."

Dolan must have lost it when he saw Nolan drop the bankroll and take my hand to escort me to the exit. He followed us.

"She doesn't know who she wants. She fucks me every chance she gets."

"She's your wife, man. That's no surprise."

"She's a slut."

"Why are you calling me out my name?" I cried.

"If you hadn't been sitting your lazy ass around pouring liquor down your throat, she never would have fucked me," Nolan spat before Dolan could answer me. "Let's go, Darica."

Dolan followed us to the parking lot, where the argument got more heated. I tried to walk as fast as I could, but my legs seemed to be frozen stiff. After we were safely in the car and I had my seat belt on, Nolan started up the ignition and drove as fast as he could toward home.

"I'm so sorry," he said.

"Don't be sorry. It comes with the territory. I knew Dolan was going to be mad, but truth be told, I never thought he'd be like this."

"Neither did I," Nolan said. "My brother was always the quiet one."

"Well, he's definitely showing his true colors now."

"I still feel really bad about this."

"If I were you, I wouldn't take full responsibility. It was just as much Dolan's idea for you to be the donor as it was yours, and when we decided to do it the 'natural way,' I was as enthusiastic as you. I could've stopped it, but I got to thinking about all kinds of things right before we made love."

"Like what?"

"Mostly selfish things like me having a child, me being a mother, me finally feeling like a real woman, me getting an orgasm. I knew you were going to bring it, and I wanted to try it just as much as you. The almighty 'me' got me in a world of trouble, and I'm definitely paying for it now. There. I said it."

"I'm glad you did. I'm proud of you. It takes a lot to be honest."

"I wish Dolan would do it. He acts like he never did anything wrong."

"I'll say."

"As a matter of fact, you did me a favor."

"What?" Nolan asked as he looked at me as if I were crazy.

"I need to confess something to you. Something that happened to me a long time ago that effected my marriage long before you came along."

"Darica, you don't have to punish yourself—"

"Please. I have to get this off my chest before it eats me alive."

"Okay," he said as he began to drive at a much-slower pace.

I told him the story about my dad, about my mother and her husband, and about the dilapidated house Ben parked me near on the night of my sixteenth birthday. I told him about the champ and what he did to me. Nolan looked at me like he couldn't believe what he was hearing come out of my mouth. But, nevertheless, he let me have my say. When I was done, he told me he was sorry that I had to endure that at such a young age and apologized for allowing the champ to come back into my life and cause me so much stress.

"Did he hurt you?" Nolan asked.

"Yes, he did," I admitted. Nolan hit the steering wheel so hard, I thought it was going to break in two, so I felt it necessary to clarify. "He traumatized my body, but he didn't really hurt it. He hurt my feelings, he hurt my pride, and he hurt my ability to feel comfortable in a sexual relationship."

"I'm not trying to be funny, but you seem to be okay."

"Well, that's where you come in. You see, there's only been two men, you and Dolan, who I've ever been sexually open with, and, please, believe me, there haven't been too many others to compare to. I know that sounds terrible coming out of my mouth right now, but I have some issues when it comes to opening up sexually. Dolan was so engrossed in having a baby that, sometimes, he forgot that I needed extratender loving care in order to feel good about myself. He forgot how much I needed foreplay and basically forgot about my needs. When I was with you, you took the time to make me feel special, made me feel loved in a way I had never felt, and even gave me something to loosen me up. Some people need things to help them get over the edge without being judged, and I am one of them. I'm not saying Dolan was boring or insensitive. I'm just saying that, sometimes, people forget what the people in their lives need most, and they judge them about the way they need it. I love my husband with all my heart and soul, but if I had it to do over again, our sex life would have been different. You feel me?"

"Yes. But I don't know what to say. I'm floored and flattered that you think that, but I've always taken the extra time to make sure the woman felt comfortable before moving a step forward, and I've always been open enough to give her what she needed in the relationship, whether it was sexual or just a platonic friendship."

"Not too many men are like that. Thank you."

"I'm glad you got that off your chest, but now, we're back to the original problem, Ben and the champ."

"I wouldn't worry myself about it," I told him. "I have an idea that's going to help."

"I don't even want them coming around you. I can't understand how your mother allowed that man to drive you around. He was a drug abuser, for God's sake."

"Yes. My mother is special. She changed so much after Daddy left, and she definitely didn't have the money she did when he was around. The champ paid them good money to accept him, but they didn't have to sell me out to do it."

"That's for damn sure," Nolan said as he held me and allowed me to cry on his shoulder.

In the absence of any real marriage or even a relationship, for that matter, Nolan did great as a fill-in. He pampered me, bought all my groceries, catered to my cravings, and treated me like a human being in a world where no one else did. I lapped it up like the ice cream I often asked him to bring me home. Some people would say that I should have cut him off, left him by the wayside, pushed him to the side like the bad omen that he ended up being in my life, but when you're pregnant and no one thinks you're right, no one treats you with respect or even gives you love, for that matter, you suck it up like a sponge whenever you can find it. I wasn't about to deal with my mother or even act or pretend that I accepted Ben, so Nolan was most definitely that guy. Nolan had become my companion, my confidant, and my friend. It wasn't good what we were doing. It wasn't good with what we had done, but we had already figured out it wasn't the most ideal situation, so we worked with what we had.

I was preparing for my baby shower and contemplating if I wanted to go to the annual masquerade ball that Rolanda and Phillip gave every year. One of my favorite singers, Delisha Mathews Broadus, was going to be there, and I didn't want to miss it. But, on the other hand, I didn't want to look as humiliated as I had been feeling. It was Nolan's idea for us to go together. It wasn't the nicest thing to do, and I was sure it was going to piss Dolan off, but, at this point, I didn't even care. He had treated me like the scum of the earth, and every time I looked at him, I felt like it too. Nolan bought us new outfits, even though I only told him I would *think* about it, and I asked Nuni to help me decide. I should have known what he was going to say.

"Girl, please. I would walk into that masquerade party and *own* that shit. Dolan walked into a restaurant with not one but *two* bitches and turned up his nose at you like you were a stranger. Trust and believe, you need to get his ass back!"

"It's not a competition, Nuni."

"Hell if it ain't. His ass needs to be cussed out, fussed out, and dogged out for what he did. You are *still* his wife, and his ass had a lot of nerves. So what you fucked his brother. It's not like the shit is unheard of, and furthermore, if he had been doing *his* job, you wouldn't have done it in the first place. Second, his ass is out there, acting like a porn star, but he expects you to do differently. At least, you slept with *one* man—not ten. And you only did it once."

"Nuni, how do you know how many times I did it?"

"Girlfriend, I know. You're better than me. If I were pregnant and my hormones were going crazy, I would definitely be fucking Nolan."

"Thanks for your advice, Nuni," I giggled. "I'll definitely consider it."

"Please do."

"Are you going?"

"Hell yeah. I'm not missing out on an opportunity to be seen in a bomb-ass outfit and a mask."

"You're so funny."

"I know. Talk to you later, girlfriend."

"Goodbye."

I woke up at six o'clock in the morning to the smell of bacon and eggs. Before I could wipe the sleep out of my eyes, Nolan was bringing in a tray.

"For my babies," he said as he flashed a winning smile, picked up a fork, and prepared to feed me.

"Wait a minute now. I'm not helpless. I can feed myself," I said while grabbing the fork and stuffing eggs in my mouth. I inhaled his heavenly cologne at the same time I swallowed. Damn, he looked good with nothing on but a pair of pajama pants. If I didn't know any better, I would swear he was trying to seduce me. It was working too. My panties were drenched.

"What's on the agenda for today?" he asked.

"Nothing much. I just plan to lounge around the house."

"Can we play Monopoly?"

"Sure. But you're gonna lose," I told him.

"We'll see about that."

"Feeling lucky?" I said as I cleaned up my plate.

"I love you," he said.

"Don't do that," I demanded.

"I can't lie. You're everything to me." I shoved the tray at him and grabbed my orange juice to gulp down.

"It's a shame."

"What?"

"A sexy man like you is ready for love, and it's with the wrong woman."

"One day you'll eat those words," he told me.

"It won't be today," I promised. "Let me get in this shower."

"I'll go get the game," he said.

Brandon

As soon as Delisha gave me the address to the place where she was performing, I cringed. She was scheduled to sing at a masquerade ball, and she wanted me to check it out to make sure it was legit. She had been kidnapped by a lunatic from her past who owned a club called Taboo. He used masks to conceal the identities of his entertainers and patrons and ended up scarring her for life. She didn't want anything to do with a mask, but she couldn't say no to the people who requested her, either. Even though the job paid well, this wasn't about money at all. She had dropped about twenty albums and was one of the highest-paid singers in the industry. But she wanted to be that all-around entertainer that stayed in touch with the world, not driven by greed, but also down-to-earth enough to get her hands dirty from time to time. So, she vowed to do at least two private engagements a year to stay connected with her fans.

How did a small-time sanitation worker end up managing one of the baddest women in the music industry? I guess you could say I was at the right place at the wrong time.

Delisha Mathews was singing at the Fish Bowl, the biggest auditorium in Belle, when a group of kids decided to cut the main supply of water to the building. Not only did the toilets stop flushing, but the purification to all the water fountains and soda machines went out, causing a major backup in the surrounding areas. Security caught two of the young thugs who happened to be bragging about what they did and the other three coming out of an underground outlet.

I happened to have arrived about two hours before showtime, called in the emergency, then went to work diagnosing the problem and requesting backup supplies and workers within minutes. In less than an hour, I had two of the snack stands and almost all the bathrooms fully operating. I rearranged the sound system and placed makeshift barriers to prevent water damage.

Delisha and her husband wanted to personally thank the man behind the scene that saved her concert. We talked until fifteen minutes before showtime and, somehow, they asked me about my musical and engineering background. They offered me a job managing part time. It paid ten times more than my sanitation gig. I took it. The rest, as they say, was history.

A butler flung the door open, snatching me back to the present, and I was very pleased because I had chickened out five times before knocking on the door. Less than two minutes after I informed him of the nature of my visit,

I found myself staring into the eyes of the one that got away.

"What the hell do you want, Brandon?" Ro said with venom.

I handed her my business card, which had a picture of Delisha and about three phone numbers. She eyed me suspiciously and invited me in. She knew there was no way in hell I could've made this up. "We meet again," I smiled.

"I guess so," she said but didn't crack a grin. She obviously failed to see the humor in it.

Miko

Dr. Ross spent thirty minutes trying to calm me down. She was working with me diligently about controlling my temper, and up until now, it was successful. I'd heard about Dolan and his breakup with his wife, despite his efforts to save the marriage. The part that made me mad wasn't so much the fact her ungrateful ass had slept with someone else. If I had a man like Dolan, another man couldn't get me to breathe on him, let alone allow him to dick me down. I would latch on to Dolan so tightly that he would swear I was a Band-Aid clinging to him like he was a kid with a scraped knee.

It wasn't even that he was so broken up that he started screwing around with bitches all across the globe. I could also handle that. But what burned me up was the fact Carlena's ass thought screwing him was the thing to do, even though she knew it took everything in me to keep from opening a can of whoop ass on her from day one, circa 2004, when she did it the first time.

"OK, Miko," Ross said when she saw how angry I was and how erratic my breathing had become. "Let's go over this again. Since we last met, the love of your life, Dolan, and his wife are on the verge of divorce, she's expecting a baby from another man, and he's gotten another woman pregnant."

"Bingo. Except for the last part. There's no way in hell Cee's carrying Dolan's baby. I feel sorry for his wife, though. Maybe she has PTSD like me or went crazy or something.

"Why do you think that?" Ross asked.

"A couple of months ago, she was stabbed in the back. I think Carlena's crazy ass did it. Then a few weeks ago, I heard she was beat up by a group of women."

"Stabbed in the back as in with a knife, or stabbed in the back by betrayal?"

"Double meaning. Somebody stabbed her up and left her for dead."

"That's terrible."

"I know. Even I wouldn't stoop that low."

"Do you have any evidence that your friend did it?"

"That bitch ain't no friend of mine. She messed that up a long time ago. No, I don't have proof, but I can get it. I know for a fact who ordered the beat down, though. The same bitch who paid people to beat up her boyfriend's fiancée and pushed her own sister off a building."

"Oh, no. Is she in jail?"

"Hell no, that bitch is walking around free as a bird."

"Tell me who it is so that I can call the authorities."

"If you knew who it was and how long their money is, you would realize that telling on her won't help the situation. She probably wouldn't even do any serious time."

"We have to do something."

"I plan to."

"What will you do?"

"I think I said a little too much. Forget it." I didn't mean to tell her so much, but the thought of Dolan and Carlena got me hotter than fish grease, and I got a little carried away. My friend Mina had told me in confidence (probably because she needed to get it off her chest) that she overheard Evette talking about what she did, including killing Sheila, stabbing Essence, and paying the project chicks to attack Darica, when she was paying Mina to get out of town and away from her man. Mina was scared of Evette, but I say she should have done everyone a favor and offed the bitch as soon as the money changed hands.

"That's pretty drastic," Ross said.

I could tell she was trying to figure out if I was just rambling for attention or really telling the truth. I hunched my shoulders and took a deep breath.

"So, what are you going to do now?"

"What I should have done a long time ago."

"Which is?"

"Put a stop to this madness."

Dr. Ross concluded the session, and I couldn't have been happier. Mina was back now, and I headed to her apartment. When I got there, she had company. Her friend Essence was there.

"Yes, girl, I feel like I hit the jackpot, and I owe it all to you for saving my life after that bitch left me for dead," Essence blurted.

"It was nothing. I did what anybody would have done if they saw someone bleeding on the road. You're the one that's a godsend. If I hadn't met you, I don't know what I would've done."

"You don't have to worry about Evette's ass. Not only is she not going to ask you for any money back, but she'll also never bother you again, and your friend, Darica, is safe too."

"Darica is not my friend. She's my ex-boyfriend's lover. But I'm done with him. I just want to see Evette get what's coming to her. She thinks she can do anything she wants, to whomever she wants to do it to. I want to see justice served."

"That bitch is crazy. I heard she's been stabbing folks and throwing them off buildings for a long time. She usually gets out of it by getting other people to take the rap or paying them off, but I know something about her that will stop her for good."

I wanted to see what else Essence had to say, but I heard Mina heading for the door, so I knocked on it quickly.

"Hey, girl," Mina said.

"Hey. Where've you been?"

"I was out of commission for a spell but thanks to my friend, Essence, I'm back."

"Nice to meet you, Essence. I'm Miko."

"Nice to meet you."

"I don't know if you overheard us or not," Mina said, "but we're talking about Evette's trifling ass. You want to help us take her down?"

"I'll gladly help if you throw Carlena in the mix."

"For sure."

Chapter Thirteen

Greg

I'd never been much of a talker, but some things had to be said. I know I fucked up big time, maybe even caused major damage. But in the end, I did the right thing by cutting Rella off and asking for more than one test. It turned out the baby wasn't mine, and I had to admit, I wasn't relieved. She was a sweet little girl, and I was doubtful that finding her real dad would be an easy task. Once I got over the urge to strangle Rella, I planned to sit down with her to figure out what we were going to do.

Right now, I needed some time to reflect on my life, and with Nolan and Dolan at odds with each other, I rarely had anyone to play sports or go out and drink with. Nevertheless, I decided to go to Massey's alone, not knowing I would soon come to regret that decision. Chevette walked in with her new man like she wasn't still married to me. Sure, she had served me with divorce papers, and I fully intended to take my stepmother's advice, but I hesitated to fill them out. I had to know if she was fully done with me.

I watched him escort her to a secluded table in the back, order their drinks, and proceed to whisper in her ear like they were bosom buddies. She threw her head back and laughed uncontrollably, although I was sure the motherfucker wasn't that funny. Jealousy enveloped me as I saw another man reap the benefits of the best thing that ever happened to me. I wondered if they had slept together and if she did that "little thing" with her tongue on him. Did she share her innermost thoughts and dreams with him? Did she tell him her secrets? Did he know about me and how I jeopardized our marriage?

I resisted the urge to storm over there and beat the shit out of both of them, gulped my drink, then asked for another until I could barely see without blurred vision. *Damn,* I thought. *This shit is really going down.* I knew, at some point, I would have to learn to live without her. But one thing for sure . . . I wasn't going to go out like a sucker.

I slipped out of the bar unnoticed and had miraculously made it home in one piece when I suddenly decided to drive the extra ten miles to my mother's house. When I arrived, I told her I'd had too much to drink, took the lecture she gave me, and followed her instructions to drink some coffee and go to sleep in one of the guest rooms. I made sure to drink enough coffee to stay awake because not only did I go into Chevette's room instead, I went into her walk-in closet and waited for her ass to come home.

She staggered in at three o'clock in the morning like it was the thing to do, and since Massey's closed at two, I didn't know if she had a nightcap with that lame or came straight home. I watched her sexy body as she took off all her clothes and lay on the bed buck naked. She cupped her beautiful breasts in each hand until the nipples stiffened into twin peaks.

I licked my lips as I watched her put on a show she didn't know she was giving and smiled when I saw her pussy glistening in the moonlight. I almost lost it when she inserted two fingers into her wet womanhood, but I still didn't know if she had fucked him and he failed to do his job, or if she was horny from holding out for so long. She started moaning, trying to finish herself off when I emerged from the closet.

"What the fuck?" she screamed.

"It's me, baby," I said as she tried to fight me off, whether or not she thought I was a stranger.

"Get out," she demanded, although her plea was weak, and she was still horny.

"Let me help you," I said as I stroked her hard clitoris. She didn't have the strength to push me away and allowed me to make love to her and bring her to a shuddering orgasm. She fell asleep in my arms, and I was the happiest I'd ever been in my life.

A few hours later, I felt her untangle herself from me. She started putting on a top and a fresh pair of jeans. I smiled at her. "You going to get breakfast, beautiful?"

"No. I'm getting ready to go into the guest room."

"I thought we were going to cuddle."

"Why would you think that?"

"After we made love, I thought we were going to announce we're back together again."

"Hell no."

"What do you mean, no? You still love me—don't you?"

"Whether or not I do, all we did was relieve some stress, *not* make love. Thank you. I needed that."

"Wait. I gave you my all. I haven't fucked around with anyone. I dumped Rella, and the DNA test came back negative. I want us to get back together."

"Good for you, but I'ma need you to sign those papers. I don't want this marriage anymore."

"Fuck," I said as I got up and started putting on my clothes.

"Can you turn the lights and radio off on your way out?" she asked as she walked out the door.

Darica

It was no coincidence that Dolan was acting so ugly at Chez Mizelle. He had signed the paperwork and made the payment to buy the restaurant hours before we had the altercation, and with that new deal in place, he became more obnoxious than ever. He made sure that everyone within earshot knew what his wife and brother did and how angry he was about it.

Whenever Nolan and I went out, whether it was to eat, go to the cleaners, or simply to get gas, it seemed like Dolan was around to berate us and make us feel bad about our deed. If I didn't know any better, I would even go so far as to say Dolan was stalking us. Nolan didn't seem fazed by it, but I was livid. It seemed as if Nolan and Dolan had done a complete one-eighty, with Nolan being the nice brother, and Dolan, well, I didn't know what category he fell in. But he was most definitely different.

There were times when I wanted to curse Dolan out, but as soon as I fixed my mouth to do it, I would feel guilty and shake my head. My husband had a way of making me feel like he was justified in what he was doing, and we were as wrong as two left shoes. One day after we arrived home from a fight with Dolan at a store, Nolan gave me a tired and frustrated look.

"Can you do me a favor?" he asked.

"Sure. What is it?" I questioned him.

"I don't care who said it or how they say it, what you've done or how bad you feel about it, but don't ever let anyone make you feel less than who you are. Promise me that."

"Well, I—"

"Promise me," he cut me off. "I don't want to hear any more about what you've done to Dolan. I'm not going to listen to any more of his rants, and I need you to back me. Everybody knows what we did. We all are paying for our sins. But life goes on. You can't keep beating yourself up about it, and nobody has a right to judge you. So, when

I say that I want you to hold your head up high, I mean every word. Do you hear me?"

"Yes," I said with confidence. With that, Nolan picked up the phone, dialed Dolan's number, and, to our surprise, he answered.

"What's up, Judas?"

"Hey, man. The name is Nolan," he corrected his brother. "I'm calling you because I don't appreciate that shit you did today."

"I don't care," Dolan said so loudly, I heard him through the phone.

"I know you don't, but let me just say this. When you see me in public with my woman, don't fucking say shit to her."

"*Your* woman?"

"Yes. She's pregnant, and it's my job to protect her and the twins at all cost. You've made it very clear that it's not your fight anymore, so I'm declaring it mine."

"What?" Dolan yelled.

"You heard me, man. Darica and I are together, and if you got a problem with her, you got a problem with me. End of discussion," Nolan said before disconnecting the call.

I knew why he did it, and I wouldn't lie; I was a little uneasy about him doing it, but I was glad it was done. I felt like I finally had an ally, somebody to take up for me, even if it was the man who had allegedly got me in this predicament in the first place. Besides, I knew my children needed an upstanding male figure in their life.

"Thank you, Nolan."

"No thanks are needed," he said. "Dolan needs to be put in his place sometimes."

"Amen to that," I agreed. Dolan hurt me to the core, and Nolan was the only one who seemed to care. I don't know if I did it out of gratefulness, felt indebted, or horny, but

I reached over to hug him; then we kissed, and one thing led to another, and we ended up in his bed making love, again. It was intense, deep, passionate, and different. I didn't stop to wonder if it was a mistake. I didn't care. It just felt right.

Dolan

Carlena was on her knees, trying her best to give me a blow job. She had on a loud-ass Mariah Carey CD, and it irked my soul. If she wasn't blasting her music as loud as all get-out, she was most definitely trying to sing the songs with the singer. I guess nobody told her she sounded like a sick cat that couldn't hold a note if it had a handle on it, and the artist was doing just fine without her killing the song.

"Stop."

"What's the matter, baby? Don't you like it? Just tell me how you want it, and I'll do it right."

"I'm not feeling this right now."

"Do you want me to get on top?"

"Hell no."

"Then what is it?" I got ready to answer her question when "Endless Love" came on.

"Turn it off."

"Yes, daddy," she said without hesitation as she jumped up and hit the power button on the CD player. By the time she turned back around, I had pulled up my pants and was fastening the buckle. The disappointment on her face was apparent. "You want anything special for dinner?" she asked as if she were my wife.

"No. I'm going to the restaurant. I don't know if I'll be back. Stop calling me daddy," I told her. "We're not related." I grabbed my keys, headed out the door, and felt the cool, crisp air hit my face, instantly giving me a sense of relief. I had to get out of there. It felt like the walls were closing in on me, and I was suffocating. I had quit my job at the insurance company, bought a hot new restaurant, and had women falling all over me, yet nothing seemed to be right in my life. It seemed like the one element I didn't have was the very thing that would make everything okay. Darica finally agreed to sign the divorce papers, and I should have had some closure, but the fact that our marriage was over sent me a message that we had failed at all we set out to accomplish. Not only were we on the brink of a divorce, but we were also both expecting babies from entirely different people.

Carlena's ratchet ass didn't know it, but I was getting a DNA test as soon as it was feasibly possible. She must've forgotten about Carlos when she tried to pin that baby on me. The only reason I was even playing with the notion of it being mine was because I wanted to hold on to the fantasy of being a father. Even with the knowledge that I could create a baby, I was so not anxious to go out and test the waters. So, Carlena's little game worked perfectly right now.

I jumped in my Lamborghini, put in my Tupac CD, blasted the music as loud as I could, backed the car out of the driveway nice and easy, then put it in drive and peeled out of there so fast, there had to be a cloud of smoke and burnt rubber in the air. My flask was full, so I gulped a swig of the Jack like it was water. It burned my throat some, but I welcomed it with open arms. I needed to lose myself in something besides pussy. While it was always good, it wasn't what I craved at the time.

Twenty minutes later, I pulled up to Chez Rogiers, formerly Chez Mizelle, jumped out, and handed the keys to one of the young waiters who was always eyeing my ride.

"Park my baby for me," I said with a smile as I staggered out of the vehicle.

"Gladly," he said as he tried to grab for my keys. I pulled them back before he could grasp them.

"Don't crash my shit," I warned him.

"No, sir," he assured me.

Darica

I was having the most relaxing bubble bath I had taken in ages . . . when every pregnant woman's nightmare happened. I didn't care how they felt or how many times they said it would never happen to them . . . Taking a bath while pregnant when home alone was *never* a good idea.

Nolan had just left to go to the grocery store. He knocked on the bathroom door to ask me if I needed anything. I said no and assured him that I was just going to take a quick shower. But I couldn't resist the temptation, and I basked in the tub for about fifteen minutes. Once the bubbles were gone, and the water was cold, the thrill passed, and I wanted out. Try though as I might, I couldn't pull myself free, and it felt like my butt was a suction cup that didn't want to let go of its porcelain counterpart. I thought about April's threat and how she jinxed me by saying she wouldn't help me get my fat ass out of the tub, when the thought suddenly occurred to me that I didn't set my phone close enough to grab it to call for help. Even if I had, she would be the last person to call on my list.

It was a good thing Nolan came back early after forgetting his grocery list. I was fit to be tied and yelling and screaming from wanting to be out of that tub so badly. Nolan busted into the unlocked door and giggled as he pulled me up out of the watery nuisance.

"If you tell April about this, I'll kill you."

"Your secret's safe with me," he said as held me up with his right hand and grabbed a towel with his left. Embarrassed was an understatement. I was hoping I could say or do something that would make Nolan forget what just happened.

"I'll do anything you say if you let me rub your stomach."

"Deal," I said as I placed his hands on my swollen belly. One of the babies kicked, and its tiny foot looked like it was trying to pierce my skin.

"Damn. Little man, don't abuse me. Your mom's the one that hasn't fed you, little kicker."

"How do you know it's a boy? Girls play football too."

"I'll put them both on a team," he laughed.

"Thank you."

"For what?"

"For letting me share this experience with you. Thank you for not letting us be homeless. I was going to leave a long time ago, but I hate to see a grown man cry."

"Funny."

"I'm just kidding."

"I know. I might pout a bit, but I wouldn't cry. I will admit, I'd be devastated without you."

"I'd miss you more."

"Really?"

"Yes, and the truth is I love having you around, and we need you."

"You do?"

"Yes."

"Thank you for being open about it, sweets."

"You're welcome," I said as I opened my arms for a hug, which he hurriedly gave me.

"Why do you call me that?"

"Call you what?"

"Sweets."

"It's a long and complicated story."

"I'm listening."

"There's this ice-cream parlor downtown owned by a friend of mine named Scotty. Scotty's wife loved the gelato with the pieces of caramel candy mixed in it almost as much as you do. She couldn't pronounce it, so she simply called it Sweets. Scotty wanted to make the place more popular, give it a bang, and have something for the customers to do while they waited. So, he started having a karaoke night. Somewhere along the way, the song, 'Sweet Thing' by Chaka Khan, became popular, so Scotty started offering $100 to whoever sang the song the best.

"You should've seen the lengths people would go through to get that money. They didn't have the best voices, but some of them were just as animated, funny, and crazy as all get-out. When you told me you had a craving for ice cream, the first place I thought to go was Scotty's. He eventually changed the name to Sweets and Karaoke. Even when you took a liking to the ice cream, I wasn't sure if that was an appropriate nickname, but the funny thing was, you kind of taste like that ice cream. That nailed it for me."

"Oh, really?"

"No lie. Listen, I need to pick up a part in Rake County. Will you be okay, or do you want to come with?"

"Isn't it a six-hour drive?"

"Yes."

"Forget it. I'm too lazy to take the trip. My back has been hurting lately. I think I need a new bed."

"I should be back around midnight. But you have to promise me you'll behave, or I won't go."

"I promise."

"You won't get into trouble or go into early labor?"

"Hell no," I said as I shooed him away.

"Good. Take my bed. You're always saying how it's more comfortable. When I get back, I'll just sleep in one of the guest rooms. We'll go bed shopping tomorrow."

"You sure?"

"Positive."

I fixed a quick dinner, and Nolan headed out. I ate a huge piece of cake and got right in his big, comfy, California King bed.

Chapter Fourteen

Dolan

"Will you be greeting some of the customers, sir?" my manager asked. I hadn't fired any of the old employees or hired new ones.

"No. That's what I pay you for."

"Yes, sir," he smiled.

I saw two waitresses in the cut next to my office and waved to them as I headed to my desk. I looked back when I was closing the door, and they were still watching me.

"Fine ass," I heard one of them say.

"That he is."

"If he's single, he can get it."

"He can get it if he's married. He's getting a divorce, though."

"Damn. Must be nice."

"I don't think he's on the market. He's too addicted to booze and pussy, in that order."

"Well, that's nothing a good woman can't fix."

I ignored the rest of their conversation because the overhead music blared Mariah Carey, and my mind started racing. My brother was living my life with the woman and family I wanted, and I had handed them to him on a silver platter.

I jumped up and almost fell back down, then scrambled for my car keys until I realized I handed them to someone to park the car. I raced down the hallway to the exit and looked for the waiter. He appeared out of nowhere.

"Man, that car rides so smoothly."

"You have my car?"

"Well, yeah."

"Give it to me."

"I just parked it."

"Man, get my car."

As soon as he pulled my car up front, I damn near shoved him on the ground and jumped in. I was driving like a madman, running lights and barely avoiding collisions. I heard cars screeching, and horns blowing, and had there been any police in sight, I was sure they would've pulled me over. I could see us in a high-speed chase with me refusing to stop because I had one goal only—to get to my wife. This separation had dragged on long enough, and I was determined to end it right now.

Nolan's door was locked, but I reached under the mat for the key I knew was there. Old habits die hard, and my brother had continued the tradition. The CD player was blaring "Endless Love," and I knew Darica had me on her mind.

I made my way up to what appeared to be Darica's room, but it was empty. I searched three guest rooms and finally happened upon Nolan's room. Darica was sleeping soundly in his bed. I almost cried when I saw her. I fell to my knees.

"Why?" I asked no one in particular. I only saw her car in the driveway, but at that moment, I didn't care if Nolan was there or not. I climbed into bed beside her and spooned her small body, rubbed her huge belly, and fought the urge to kiss it.

"Dolan, what are you doing here?" she asked when she saw my wedding ring.

"Darica!" I yelled. "You smell so good. What are you doing in this bed?" She stirred, then froze, took a deep breath, and rolled over to face me. I could tell she was horrified.

"Dolan?" she said again.

"In the flesh," I slurred.

"I thought I was dreaming. How did you get in this house?"

"Do you think of me when you make love to him?"

"Nolan and I don't make love; we're friends. I'm only in his bed because it's comfortable, and he's not here."

"I believe you. Come home with me, right now."

"What home? You sold it."

"I bought you a new one. I need you, baby."

"Dolan, you're drunk."

"A drunk mouth speaks the sober truth. I can't let my brother take you from me."

"If that's what this is about, I'm not going anywhere with you."

"Yes, you are. You love me," I said as I attempted to grab her and lift her out of bed. She was kicking, and I was already unsteady. We fell back on the bed. I didn't know if she was afraid I was going to fall on her, drop her, or if she just changed her mind, but she agreed to go with me. She grabbed her purse off the nightstand and took my hand. I almost broke my neck running out of the house, not bothering once to close the door or look back.

Nolan

I was exhausted, but I wanted to bring Darica something home. I stopped at a twenty-four-hour grocery store and got her some gelato ice cream. It wasn't her favorite, but it would do. I placed the ice cream, along

with the ring I bought in Rake County, on the passenger
seat, so I had easy access to it when I got home. When I
pulled into the driveway, I almost had a heart attack. My
front door was wide open! At first, I thought something
happened, and I screamed out.

"Darica!"

When I got no answer, I went into her room, and when
I didn't find her there, I remembered she was in my bed
and ran in there. The only sign that she was ever in there
was the unmade bed and her scarf. The sheets were
slightly pulled off the mattress like someone tried to pull
her out and she resisted.

The first thing I thought was someone tried to rob the
place and took her with them when they left. I cursed
myself for being so arrogant that I didn't protect her by
getting an alarm system or a dog. I thought I was all she
needed. I sat on the bed, wondering if I missed any signs
like a ransom note, wondered if I should call the police,
when I thought to look for her purse and cell phone. Both
were missing, so I decided to call her. My heart was doing
flip-flops in my chest as I listened to her phone ring three
times. I was almost about to hang up when she answered.

"Hello."

"Oh my God, Darica. Are you okay?"

"Yes."

"Thank God. When I came home, the door was flung
open, and I found the bed unmade. I thought something
happened to you."

"I'm fine. I'm sorry I left such a mess."

"It's fine, as long as you're okay. You must be at April's.
What time is she bringing you home?"

"No, I'm not with April."

"Are you with Chevette or Nuni?"

"No."

"Are you at your mother's?"

"No."

"I'm running out of options, sweets."

"Nolan—"

"Yes?" I anxiously asked.

"I'm with Dolan."

I felt bile rise in my throat and felt like throwing up.

"Please tell me you did not say what I think you said."

"I'm sorry, Nolan."

"It's okay. I'm coming to get you."

"Nolan, I—"

"That son of a bitch is really off his rocker taking you off like that—"

"Nolan—"

I was in my car and speeding down the highway before she could say another word. I heard her screaming my name through the phone, but I didn't want to talk. I had to get to her. Only one thing mattered to me, and it was getting her out of my brother's grip. As unstable as he was these days, there was no telling what he'd do to that woman, and with her being pregnant, I knew she couldn't fight him off.

I drove so fast, it was a wonder I made it anywhere in one piece. I ran every light and stop sign like someone in my family was dying, but *I* was the one that was dying—dying to get to my baby. The only woman I'd ever loved with a passion so intense, it would make me go to the home of a man whose blood ran through my veins.

When I got there, I didn't even bother to take the key out of the ignition. I left the car running, sprinted up to the door, and almost broke it off the hinges from banging and knocking so hard. In my mind, I had convinced myself that Dolan had abducted his own wife from my house while I was gone after waiting for the perfect opportunity, then pounced on her and took her when she was most vulnerable. I had convinced myself that she was mine—

that everything we went through and everything we were going through was my fight, and, in the end, I would be victorious and have the prize.

But the one thing I didn't count on was the fact that Darica felt she was bound to another, had signed a lifelong contract with my brother. I had eaten with him, grew up in the same household with him, fought over bathrooms, toys, and attention, and, yet, I didn't regard the one thing he had that I felt entitled to. It was as if he had fucked up so badly that I'd used it as an excuse to pass judgment, give him his sentence, and, in the end, decided to banish him from his wife.

I, the man who had always loved multiple women, didn't care whether they came or left, didn't care whether I had them or not, didn't give a shit what happened in their lives once I got what I wanted. But now, what I wanted more than anything was love, plain and simple. It was what I was looking for, the missing link in my life. Unfortunately, it was in the form of a woman I couldn't have. I couldn't accept that, so, when I saw Dolan, I punched him in the face, wanted to tear his heart out, wanted to beat him senseless for hurting her all those times, and it didn't even occur to me that it was not my place.

"What the hell's the matter with you?" he said as he held his jaw.

"You took Darica."

"I didn't *take* anything. I came over to your house and asked *my* wife if she wanted to get back together. She said yes, and, now, we're at *our* house minding *our* own business, and *you're* trespassing."

"What the hell are you saying? Darica wouldn't get back with you."

"Oh yeah? Why don't you ask her? Darica!" he yelled into the house. "Come to the door and tell Nolan that we are back together." I just knew he was lying. I stood there defiantly with my arms crossed over my chest, waiting for her to come to the door. I didn't know what I thought she was going to say, but I just knew she was going to say what I wanted to hear. I looked at her face and saw pain, hurt, and anguish. She looked like this was the worst moment in her life, like she was being asked to give an impromptu speech that she was ill-prepared for. "Tell him," Dolan said. "Tell this man that you are back with your husband so that he can go on with his life."

She coughed, took a deep breath, and sniffled. I saw the tears falling down her face. She could barely look me in the eye, let alone form any words, but here she was about to tell me something, and it seemed like the words were never going to come out of her mouth. She spoke in slow motion, and it almost seemed like she wasn't speaking at all. Only the things that eventually did come out of her mouth defied any law I had ever studied. Being a neurosurgeon for so many years had taught me to read faces, and what I read on hers was pure hell. She stood up straighter, leaned against the doorway for support, took another breath, and looked me in the eye.

"Nolan," she said, "Dolan and I are going to work on our marriage."

"What?" I blurted. "I thought you were getting a divorce. You have the papers at home."

"About those," Dolan interrupted. "She won't be needing them. I have copies here, but she tore them up."

"Is this true?" I asked her. She nodded that it was. "After he did all that shit to you? After he fucked all those women? After he started back drinking? You can't tell me you're going to work on anything with him because he's an asshole, and you don't want him, sweets."

"Because I love my wife so much, I'm going to forget about that little nickname you gave her and try to forgive both of you for your indiscretions, but I *am* going to need you to leave our house *right now*."

"Fuck you, man," Nolan said. "Darica's coming home with me."

"Read my lips," Dolan blurted. "She's *not* your wife; she's mine, and we say we're going to work it out. You're in the way, and you need to step back."

"Can we have a minute?" Darica asked her husband. "I just need to talk to him alone for a second, please."

"You have five minutes," Dolan said. "After that, I'm calling the cops to have him thrown off my property."

I ignored his remark, grabbed Darica's hand, and walked with her to my car.

"Please reconsider what you're doing right now," I pleaded. "He can't take care of you, he can't take care of the twins—he can't even fucking take care of himself. Look at this place. He bought a restaurant, and he can't even run that. You don't have to come home with me. I'll get you a hotel room or buy you another house, but you can't stay here with him. It's never going to work."

"Nolan, I'm not stupid. This is *my* marriage, and I need to try to make it work. I can't just leave my husband."

"Like he left you? Like he screwed around with all those women?"

"But he didn't fuck my sister."

"I don't care if you never get with me. I don't care if you never make love to me again. I don't even care if you don't talk to me anymore in life, but please, don't go back to Dolan. He's not right, honey. He can't do it for you. Let him get some help and *then* reconsider saving your marriage."

"I would think you'd be happy for me. You said you were my friend, even said that you loved me, but you don't. You're just thinking about yourself. You don't want my marriage to work; you don't care what happens to the twins; all you can think about is you."

"That is so not true, and you know it. I just want what's best for you, what's best for the kids."

"Then let me do this. It's what I want."

"Are you sure?"

"I'm positive."

"Fine, good luck. Call if you need me. I mean it."

"Thank you so much. Don't worry about me. I'll be fine."

"Okay."

"Nolan?"

"Yes?"

"I'm sorry about everything."

I kissed her on the forehead and walked back to my car, feeling like my soul was crushed into a million pieces.

Darica

After Nolan left, I felt like crap. I never wanted to hurt him, and I would always hate myself for that. On the other hand, I was back with my husband, and I finally felt relieved. He had told me he sold the house, and the sale was almost complete, but he would see what he could do to stop it. Most of our belongings were packed up and in storage, but he had a brand-new house for us to live in.

"Let's take a quick nap, and then we'll drive to the new house," he promised. I woke up to Dolan throwing up in the bathroom. His phone was ringing off the hook, and he obviously wasn't going to answer it. For some reason, I felt a sense of foreboding. I got up and got me a glass of water, went to the window, and looked out at what used to be my garden. There was nothing but weeds and shrubs. At that moment, I wondered how he even sold the house. Dolan came out of the bathroom, rinsed his mouth in the sink, and splashed cold water on his face.

"You're going to love the new house," he said as we heard a knock at the door. We both walked up to answer it. Carlena stood there in disbelief.

"What is *she* doing here?" she asked.

"This is *my* house, and *I'm* back."

"Dolan, what the fuck is your problem? How could you take her back after all she's done to you? I'm pregnant with your child. Doesn't that count for *anything?*"

"First of all, bitch, you better be glad I'm pregnant because if I weren't, I'd beat your ass. *You're* the reason my husband and I broke up in the first place."

"What's she talking about?" he asked Carlena as she started backing away.

"Nothing. She's just tripping."

I took a few steps toward her and slapped the shit out of her. She held her face and started trembling. Dolan got in between us.

"You two need to cut that out," he said. I was about to tell Dolan everything she did when a car pulled up. It was my doctor.

"Dr. Winters."

"Hello, Darica."

"Is everything okay?"

"Yes. I'm here to see Carlena."

"Carlos, why did you follow me? I told you I didn't want anything more to do with you."

"That's *my* baby you're carrying, and you know it."

"In your dreams. I don't want you, Carlos. I love Dolan."

"That man ain't thinking about you."

"Amen to that," I told them. "You may as well go with Dr. Winters because your ass will get cobwebs waiting for Dolan to touch you again."

"Get out, Carlos."

"So, it's like that? After all I've done for you, wrote fake prescriptions, botched up test results, got fired from jobs, and almost lost my license—*this* is how you repay me?" I looked around for Dolan, but he was nowhere to be found. I figured he went to the bathroom to throw up again. He came back with a prescription bottle, and the next thing we knew, he was choking the hell out of Dr. Winters.

Chapter Fifteen

Dolan

I tried to choke the shit out of that motherfucker. He was behind my fertility issues, and, somehow, I knew Carlena was in on it too. She looked horrified, and once she helped Darica pry my hands off the good doctor's neck, she put him in her car and drove away. After the shit they pulled, I doubted they would call the police, but I grabbed Darica to take her to the new house, just in case. I had to figure out our next move, and I was so shaken up, it was hard for me to concentrate.

Darica gasped when we pulled up to a five-bedroom, three-bath home, that, lucky for me, my parents had purchased years ago. I had been too full of pride to accept it then, but I now knew I had to do something to show my wife I wanted to work things out and take care of her and the kids. It wasn't a mansion but would suffice for our family. There was a lot of truth in what Nolan said, but I was not about to let him show me up. He'd never been married and didn't know the first thing about keeping a woman. That's why I had my wife back, and we were on our way to happiness. I knew more than anybody that I needed help for my problems, but at this point, I was taking one day at a time. I felt everything would fall into place since I had her back.

Darica was pleased to see that the house was furnished, and she had everything she needed, including her own office. I knew about her losing her job and how devastating that had to be, but I told her for years that she was a true artist, and her interior decorating business was the best thing she ever started. I made sure she would have plenty of room for all her plans, so her creative juices could flow.

"The office is beautiful, and the nursery is breathtaking."

"I knew you'd like it, baby."

"I love it."

"Go check your closet. I bought you some clothes for your birthday that you never got to see."

"Okay. Thank you, baby." She was so happy about the house that she didn't know what to do. I heard the shower running and knew she found something to wear and was anxious to show it off. I paid a pretty penny to put her in the finest threads. She came out in a purple Seraphine maternity dress, and she looked radiant.

"You look great. I hope you like the color."

"It's beautiful but so expensive."

"Nothing but the best for you, baby. I even cooked some food for you."

"Thank you," she answered but looked at it like it was the most disgusting thing she ever laid eyes on. I'd never been much of a cook, and breakfast time was long over, but I had made a feeble attempt to cook eggs, which were the only thing we had in the house. The eggs were runny, and the coffee was watery, but I hadn't drunk the stuff in ages and had forgotten the correct way to prepare it. I picked up the glass of whiskey that had replaced my coffee months ago.

"You're drinking this early in the day?" she asked.

I wanted to say something smart, but I didn't want her to get all in her feelings. "Yes, baby. I can handle it."

She looked at me like I was crazy, but I could tell she was as reluctant as me to rock the boat. She barely drank her coffee and didn't eat the eggs at all, but she devoured her toast and orange juice.

I couldn't take it any longer. I grabbed her face and kissed her passionately. "I want you right now." She nodded as I picked her up to carry her into our bedroom.

Once we arrived, I put on our song, wasted no time undressing her and diving into her hot flesh. I let my tongue dance on her erect clitoris like I was licking an ice-cream cone. She screamed my name so loudly, it scared me, and she was thrashing around so hard, I had to hold her hips down to keep her from knocking me off her. My wife came about three times and started begging for me to make love to her. I gave her what she wanted, and she cried out my name so many times, I thought somebody was going to call the police. Her pussy was always the best, but now it was so magnificent, I thought I had died and gone to heaven. I almost came about five times, but I miraculously held back so we both could enjoy the moment. I wanted our reunion to be so sweet, she would never forget it. I pumped her hot, wet mound for a few more minutes, but it was far too much to take, and I blasted so much come in her, it started gushing all over the bed. We collapsed in each other's arms sated and happy as we fell asleep.

The sun had set by the time we woke up, this time to the pounding on our door. I got up to answer it while Darica freshened up. Shit. It was Rolanda, Millie, and Mama C.

"Hey, lovely ladies," I greeted.

"Hello, son. I heard you and Darica got back together."

"I see good news travels fast. Have a seat," I said as I hugged my grandmother and Millie.

"Are you okay, love?" Millie asked after they were seated in the living room.

"Sure. Why wouldn't I be?"

"Don't get smart," Mama C said. "We just came to check on you two."

"Everything is fine, if that's what you mean. I'm sure Nolan cried you a river."

"Nolan wasn't the one that told me. April was."

"Damn. How did she know?"

"I texted her that I was coming here," Darica said as she walked in.

"Oh, great. Now, I have to hear her mouth, plus Nuni's theatrics and Chevette's rants."

"We just want what's best for you and Darica."

"Oh, so now I'm not good enough? You think she should be with Nolan?"

"Don't be defensive. Nobody said that."

"You didn't have to. That's what you're thinking. This family is whack. One minute, you want my wife with me and with Nolan in the next. I don't give a fuck what you want; it's our life." Rolanda slapped the shit out of my right cheek. I just held my hand up to my face.

"Who the hell do you think you're talking to?" she asked as she got ready to slap my left cheek.

"That's enough, Ro. He's been through a lot," Mama C commanded. "Grandson, we don't care what you do, as long as you don't continue to be as reckless as you've been the past couple of months."

"I know I have to clean up my act. I'll do right by my family, if that's what you mean."

"That's exactly what she means," Rolanda confirmed. "Darica, are you sure this is what you want?"

"Yes," she said.

"Good because I'm about to check on Nolan. This situation is way out of hand. There ain't going to be no back-and-forth. You hear me?"

"Yes, ma'am."

"I know a couple of rehab centers," Millie added, more to change the subject than anything.

"Fine. I'll get on that right away," I told them.

"Good because in case you've forgotten, I have a set of grandkids coming in a few weeks, and I'm not letting them be born into no bullshit."

"I hear you, slugger." I smiled as I referred to her hitting my face.

"Sorry, son, I had to make sure you heard me."

"I heard you loud and clear."

They got up to leave, and Darica and I hugged them and walked them to the door. Darica was still exhausted and seemed a little sad. I tucked her in bed and finished off my bottle of whiskey. The manager of the restaurant called me, so I headed over there. It was like a repeat of the day before with me barely able to drive. The only difference was I had my wife back.

After I put out the fire that the call was about, a disgruntled customer that wanted a refund, I went to my office to sit down for a bit. One of the waitresses from the other day came in, got on her knees, and gave me a blow job. I didn't know what she wanted, but at this point, I didn't care. I didn't want to do this, especially after I just got back with my wife. I tried to push the girl away, but it was feeling so good, and I didn't have much strength to stop her. I figured I would deal with it later. I let my head fall back to enjoy the moment, then pushed her away before she finished me off. She wanted to straddle me, but I didn't let her. I managed to convince myself that what she did to me so far wasn't really cheating. She was pissed off, but I assured her that whatever she wanted, I would give it to her, as long as it was reasonable. She smiled and walked out.

I polished off a half bottle of whiskey and headed home, defying the laws of traffic, gravity, and reason once again. I managed to make it home in one piece, but I wasn't happy when I got there. By the time I put my key in the door, it was too late to turn around, and I knew it was time to face the music to the tune of Nuni, Chevette, and April. They didn't hear me come in, but I heard their conversation. I knew they were giving my wife hell, and I would be less than a man if I didn't come to her rescue.

Darica

My husband never lied when he made that comment about good news. Not only was April not happy for me, she came over to personally tell me how displeased she was about it and brought help to drive the nail in the wood. As soon as I opened the door, I was interrogated by the trio, who assured me that I did not think things through before jumping back into my husband's arms. It didn't help that he was falling all over the place, and his speech was unintelligible when he walked in.

"Darica Ross Rogiers, what the hell are you doing? First, you tell us you're living with Nolan; then you flip the script and reunite with your husband."

"April, I think you're cute, but what I do with my husband is my business."

"Not when it involves my nieces or nephews in your stomach. Your husband is fucking and sucking on a lot of bitches. Did you consider *that?*"

"I'm aware."

"*Aware?*" Chevette said. "That's no joke. You should've learned something when I went through the same thing. I'm happy it's all behind me."

"Girlfriend, is everything good? I don't want you or your babies to be sick."

"Since I'm obviously not qualified to run my own life, what do you think I should do? Go back to Nolan's and say, 'Honey, I'm home'?"

"All we're saying is you need to make Dolan responsible for his actions. You don't have to go back to him. Take it slow, make him go into rehab or therapy, get tested for STDs, date for a while."

"This is some bullshit. I'm not going to waste another minute being away from my husband."

"You're in love with being in love. I know you want your marriage to work, honey, but this is *not* the way."

Dolan walked in the room and staggered over to us, damn near fell on top of Nuni, and slurred, "What the hell is zis? Can' my wife and me live our lifes without people's putting tweny cens in?"

"Boy, bye. You don't get to drag my sister through the mud and I not get involved," April told him.

"You Rogiers brothers are all alike—trifling, conniving, and horny. I left your brother because he couldn't keep his dick in his pants, and now you're over here doing the same thing to Darica."

"Here'sa li'l tip for ya. I'm not Greg. Won' you biches get ou ma house?"

"No, this motherfucker didn't!" April shouted as she made her way over to slap him.

"Girlfriend, it won't do any good," Nuni said. "He probably won't remember anything in the morning."

"He's right," Chevette said. "Darica's made up her mind, and we have to support her. That doesn't mean we're giving up on her. I'll come over here every day if I have to."

"Amen!" Nuni shouted.

"Okay," April said. "Sis, I'm not going to apologize because you know how I roll. He better do right by you," she threatened.

Dolan just looked at her angrily and opened the door for them. They all walked out somberly, and we went to bed.

I, once again, woke up to Dolan vomiting in the bathroom. I padded into the kitchen and found empty bottles everywhere. This was a far cry from being with Nolan and waking up to peace, quiet, breakfast, and coffee. Dolan was not going to any lengths to make me happy. There would be no breakfast in bed, no runs to the store for ice cream, and unless I took a liking to whiskey, the pantry wasn't going to fill itself. The sex was the only thing banging, and even that was questionable. I had to wonder what I was going to do once the twins were here.

Nolan

The scent of her was intoxicating. I took a deep breath to inhale more of it. She reached out her tiny hand and traced the lines of my face before parking her index finger on my lips. I sucked her finger like it was a piece of caramel candy. She raked her hand down my chest to my glistening eight-pack and continued until it landed on my rock-hard package.

The hand job alone was making me squirm, but, coupled with me gazing in her beautiful eyes, it was the best feeling in the world. She got on her knees to take me into her mouth, and I almost exploded on her tongue. She spit on my dick and jacked me off, as she bobbed up and down my shaft like she was dying to taste my seed.

Somehow, I maneuvered her into the sixty-nine position and dived into her sweet gelato. Oh my God. I never tasted anything so succulent. The way her juices poured in my mouth like a waterfall made me feel like I was in paradise. She came so hard, and so many times, I thought she was going to pass out.

"Come for me," she begged. "I want to taste you."

I happily obliged, releasing so much, I almost flooded her mouth. She swallowed and looked at me like she wanted more. I wanted to make love to her, but after giving her all that I had, I was dry as a bone. I held her against me, wanting to bask in the afterglow before speaking.

"I thought I lost you for good," I said.

"You will never lose me. I'll always be here."

"Thank you for coming back to me. You won't regret it."

"Baby, I was a fool for trying," she whispered. I tried to grab her tighter, but she was moving backward. The harder I tried to hold her, the more she was moving away from me.

"Darica! Darica! Darica!" I called out. I woke up clenching a pillow. I threw that shit across the room when I realized it was only a dream. Darica hadn't come back, she didn't just give me the best blow job I had in my life, and didn't just promise to stay with me forever. It was a fucking nightmare. I stumbled out of my bed, trembling from loss and need. I never imagined she'd be gone, never felt this kind of pain, and wouldn't wish it on my worst enemy.

All kinds of thoughts ran through my mind. I pictured her fucking Dolan, doing the same thing to him she did to me, pictured them in a new house raising the twins. That shit fucked me up in the head.

Then I thought about him dragging her through the mud, abusing her, and not valuing her worth, and I felt even worse because I knew she would sit there and take it.

If I had taught her anything, it was how precious she was and to not take shit from anyone. I cringed at the thought she loved my knuckleheaded brother more than anything in this world, would do anything to save their marriage, and he knew it. I saw the cockiness in his eyes, and it made me sick because I used to be standing in the same shoes. Dolan truly didn't know what he had, and, sadly, I played a part in turning him into that monster. I had no idea what that man must've been going through when he found out I'd violated his wife, and I had no right to judge the way he coped with it. He had turned to alcohol to drown his broken heart; he had picked his poison. Now, I had to pick mine.

I tried to suck it up and go about my day, but everything I did was a daze of meaningless animation I used to get from point A to B. The watery coffee I spilled on my shirt burned my skin underneath. Shit. It was the second shirt I put on today. I undercooked my eggs, and my toast looked more like a piece of black construction paper than food. I missed Darica so much, but more than that, I worried about her, wondering if Dolan was being the husband he promised he'd be and if things were going as good as she thought they would. I prayed that he would get help for his problem and remembered to remain patient and levelheaded with her.

I called into work, needing one more day to get myself together. With a job like mine, I would much rather not go in at all than jeopardize anyone's safety. It's crazy how devastating your life could be when you lose someone who was your world for six months. I didn't even know how to live my life without her. I fixed her breakfast, washed her hair, listened to her hopes, and even checked her vitals.

She was the sister I never had and the lover I always needed. When I was telling her the story about Sheila, I never dreamed I would love her ten times more. She sat there and listened, and she was happy for me, truly happy. I never thought anyone would root for me. I wasn't missing Darica because of the way she made me feel physically. I was missing her for what she did to my heart, and I knew there would never be another like her.

My nightmares were filled with thoughts of losing her, and my dreams were of me wishing I could turn back the hands of time. Most days, I begged God for one more day in her arms or at least a chance to be her best friend again. I knew it wasn't going to happen, definitely felt I didn't deserve it, but I was sick in my spirit and needed a lift.

I headed over to S&K for a gelato. The parking lot was full, and I had to park down the street and walk, but I felt like I needed the exercise. By the time I got there, a couple was leaving, and that left me with a table big enough for at least four. I felt bad about taking the spot, but I planned on sharing if anyone wanted to sit.

I was having a good time eating my chili cheese fries and gelato and laughing at the people bold enough to enter the karaoke contest, when a group of ladies walked in. They asked if the rest of the seats in my booth were taken when our eyes met.

"I'm sorry to bother you," Mina said. "We'll find another table."

"No problem," I assured her. "Sit down. I have plenty of room."

"Thank you," she answered.

"No problem," I said. It seemed like forever since I'd been with her, and so much had happened that it didn't even faze me. I was more enthralled by the others she was with. Miko, Essence, and Mina made quite a trio. We had a good time watching the crowd have fun, but, unfortunately, the women had to leave and handle some business, and I was all alone once again.

I was just about to go up and enter the contest when Darica walked in. Her stomach was even bigger than the last time I saw her, and she looked like she was about to drop those twins any minute. I immediately helped her into the booth. I was so happy to see her; there was no way I could express it in words. I let her do all the talking. She brought me up to speed about everything that was going on so far, and we laughed at her rendition of Nuni, April, and Mama C. The funniest part was hearing about Dolan getting smart with Rolanda and her slapping the piss out of him.

"Better go on up there," she said.

"Where?"

"I know you want to enter that contest. You practiced enough in the bathroom. It's showtime. Break a leg!"

"Thanks," I grinned. I made my way to the front, told them what key I preferred to sing in, and grabbed the microphone. I was nervous as hell, but my inspiration was sitting in a booth watching my every move, so I had to bring it on.

"I will love you anyway
Even if you cannot stay
I think you are the one for me
Here is where you ought to be."

Everyone started dancing and cheering me along, so the rest of the song was easy. Darica was right. All that practice in the shower paid off. I was a natural. As I walked back to my seat, I was a bag of nerves; even though I knew the crowd loved me, I only wanted one person's opinion. She jumped up and flung her arms around me with a knowing smile that I was singing to her.

I walked her to her car and followed her as far as possible before turning off the main road and heading home. She promised to keep in touch, and that would have to be enough for me. Being with her was like food for a starving man, and having a small taste was better than having none at all. My heart was lighter now. I went home and slept like a baby.

Mina called and woke me up at six in the morning. I was scheduled for work at eight.

I hoped she wasn't up to no funny business because if she were, I planned to tell that ass off.

"Sorry to wake you up so early, but I couldn't sleep a wink after seeing you at the restaurant."

"Why?"

"I have something to tell you about Evette and Sheila."

"You know them?"

"I know one of them by word of mouth, but the other I know very well. Can we meet up somewhere? I have to do this in person."

"Sure. I'll meet you at Chez Rogiers on my lunch break." I wasn't inviting her to my house. I learned my lesson.

Mina told me the story of Evette and Ari, and I couldn't believe my ears, but when she told me about Evette's connection to Sheila, I needed a drink. I ordered my usual and allowed her to proceed.

"I'm sorry I didn't come to you sooner. I had to get my facts in order."

"So, let me get this straight. Evette killed Sheila, and *nobody* saw it?"

"As far as we know, there were no witnesses. Ari had already left the scene, and none of the neighbors were home."

"Why haven't you gone to the police?"

"We already tried that. They investigated it as a suicide, and, of course, there was no DNA taken at her apartment. Without evidence, it's damn near impossible to connect her."

"You said she confessed it to Essence, right?"

"Yes, but who's going to believe a ratchet prostitute over a wealthy socialite?"

"Maybe I can get her to confess. I'll act like I'm happy she did it or something."

"Good luck. Not even your good loving will convince her to spend the rest of her life in prison. Even if you were to come back in her life and slowly weasel your way back into her heart, she has Payne now, and he's getting ready to marry her."

"Word?"

"Yes. She figures if she can't have you, she may as well take the next best thing. We're all doing that."

"Maybe it's just as well," I said, ignoring the comment. "If I see Evette, I'm going to hurt that woman."

"Get in line. The girls and I are on it either way."

"Thanks for the information. I feel like a ton of bricks were lifted off me."

"No problem. It felt good telling you. Thanks for the very expensive lunch."

"You're welcome. Enjoy and eat everything on that $500 plate!"

"Most definitely."

I tossed and turned all night. On one hand, I was relieved that I finally had some closure that Sheila wanted her life just as much as I always believed she did. But, on the other hand, I felt guilty that she had to die so young, especially at the hands of her own sister who was most likely jealous of her, angry at her, and was offing her because of me. It felt strange knowing that I had something so captivating that someone would want to kill to get it. I had to wonder if it was all me or was Evette just insane to the highest degree? Was she simply paying Sheila back for the sins of her parents, or the fact that she was the result of their union? Maybe it was all of the above, and Evette stopped seeing clearly a long time ago. She had damn near cut off Essence's torso, but she was lucky enough to survive. Either way, she had to pay for her crime and not be allowed to do it again.

I wanted to tell Dr. Lane, but I had to stop myself. How do you tell a man that the person who murdered his youngest child was her older sister, someone she trusted and a woman he loved even more than life itself? He would never accept it, and without proof, would probably even resent it. As much as I hated to keep this secret, I would have to hold it in until I found the evidence.

Dolan wasn't happy about me coming to his restaurant, but, hey, it was a free country. He was probably just mad that I saw him go into his office followed by a buxom, wavy-haired waitress, and I didn't miss seeing him zip up his pants when he walked out. She was wiping something off her mouth, which I was pretty sure was something he shot into it. I didn't trip because I knew without telling Darica a thing that he would fuck up royally. I was just glad she allowed me to call and check on her. That was enough for me at this point.

By the time morning came, I was ready to face a full day at work. People were waiting to be saved, and I loved doing it. I fixed myself a big breakfast, one Darica would be proud of, made myself a huge cup of coffee, and grabbed my keys. I hadn't smiled this much in a while.

Chapter Sixteen

Darica

When Nolan was singing at S&K, I saw a few women checking him out. Who could blame them? He was one of the finest men alive. I smiled as I watched him bellow the tune that he nicknamed me from. The words stopped my heart because I knew he felt every bit of the emotions inside him. I said a silent prayer that he would someday find a woman just for him and get closure to the hole I left in his broken heart.

I walked into the house later that night around ten o'clock. Dolan was sitting at the kitchen table with a bottle. He took a swig from it and stood up to meet my gaze. He staggered over to me, and in the next second, was in my face.

"What the hell are you doing coming in my house this late?"

"It's only ten o'clock."

"The only women out this late are ones with their legs open."

"I don't say anything about you coming in here late, smelling like a liquor store and pussy."

"I work around booze and women. Who the hell do you think you're talking to like that?"

"You're the only one here."

"You need to watch your mouth."

"The last time I checked, you were *not* my daddy."

"I'm your husband. Show me some respect. I'm good to you."

"In whose opinion?" I asked while walking out of the kitchen.

"Darica, don't walk away from me."

I was in our bedroom by the time he finished his sentence. He followed me to continue the fight.

"Were you with him?"

"Who?"

"My brother. I found the birthday present he gave you in the back of the closet when I was packing," he said as he threw the card at me.

I didn't have to read it. I'd never forget the words Nolan wrote:

These diamonds shine bright, but they have nothing on you. I imagined myself hugging those luscious curves when I bought this dress. I hope you think of me whenever you wear them. Happy birthday, beautiful.

Love,

Nolan

"Is he trying to take what belongs to me?" Dolan asked.

"If you have to ask, then—"

"Did you fuck him?" he interrupted.

"Go straight to hell, Dolan." I took my gown and slippers and went into the guest room.

"Uh-uh. Ain't gon' be none of that. We sleep together every night. Get your ass in this room so we can make love."

"Dolan, get your drunk ass off me." I pushed him.

"Come here."

"No. Move."

"I'm warning you, Darica. Take those clothes off and get in our bed."

"Or what?"

"Or I'll exercise my rights as your husband."

"You going to rape me?"

"No. I'm your husband. I'm entitled to have you any way I want you." He pulled me in the bed with him, and I let him have his way. I didn't enjoy it one bit and was glad it didn't take him long to come and fall asleep. I cried myself to sleep, thinking this was a terrible idea. I prayed that we would get over this setback before my babies were born.

April and Chevette came to cheer me up. They knew I wasn't feeling all that good, and they wanted to let me know what they were doing, in terms of the baby shower, so far. Nuni was on a date, but he sent in his suggestions. We decided to have it at Rolanda's in her garden. She had a new alarm system, and she was determined to test it out. God knows she was feeling some type of way when I got stabbed. She wanted to show the world all was good in her camp.

"What's going on, sis?" April asked.

"Nothing."

"I don't believe that for a minute. Is it Dolan?"

"Yes."

"Is that fool still drinking?"

"Yep."

"You need to kick his ass to the curb. He knows you're going to have the babies soon. How much time does he think he can waste?"

"I don't know, but I'm tired. He comes home all hours of the night wanting to make love, and I'm not feeling it."

"Do you think he's cheating?"

"I'm almost certain."

"See, that's the shit I hate," Chevette said. "I'm so glad I left Greg's ass."

"I never had these problems with Nolan. He took care of everything. Sometimes, I wish . . . never mind."

"What?" April said.

"I sometimes feel like I married the wrong brother."

"I wouldn't go that far, but I will say that Dolan was better when he wasn't drinking."

"You have a point, but what I can't understand is why Dolan allowed this situation to make him turn to drinking," Chevette said.

"I think he was a closet drinker already," I admitted. "I just know that if things don't start looking up, I'm leaving."

"I ain't even mad. You definitely deserve better," Chevette said.

"Do I?"

"I know you feel like Dolan has a right to do you wrong, but he doesn't. You paid for your mistakes. If he wasn't going to do right by you, he shouldn't have taken you back," April said.

"True. I wish somebody would give his ass the memo."

"Damn, Nolan, that feels so good."

"I'll always make you feel good, whether it's feeding you your favorite food or making you come."

"I know things were definitely easier when I was with you."

"The door is always open. Just come home."

"You know I can't do that. I can't leave my husband. I have to see this through until we take our last breath."

"Is that what you want? Dolan is definitely heading in that direction. If he doesn't stop drinking, he's going to be wrapped around a pole."

"He promised to get help."

Nolan didn't say anything. He just kissed my neck, slowly unbuttoned my blouse, and sucked on my breasts. I didn't try to stop him. Soon, he had all my clothes off. I watched his perfect body as he disrobed. Looking at his eight-pack was always a treat. He gently laid me down on the chaise lounge. I sucked in air as I felt his thick flesh enter me. Nolan stroked me thoroughly, making me feel every inch. I gasped at the amount of juices that gathered on his rod.

"Uuuuum. Yessssss. That feels amazing."

"You feel good too, baby. I never want to stop loving you." Suddenly, Nolan started fading away. I realized I was having another dream when I heard Chevette snoring from the opposite couch. April had already left, and I tried to put a blanket over my remaining friend, but she woke up as well, kissed me goodbye, and went home.

I didn't know what made me do it, but I called Nolan's number. He answered on the first ring.

"Everything okay, sweets?"

"Everything is fine. I just wanted to hear your voice."

"I'm glad you called. I'm always here for you. You need me to bring you anything? I know my selfish brother's not handling his end."

"No, thank you. Just talking to you makes me feel better."

"Where is Stupid anyway?" Nolan asked.

"You mean Dolan? He's in the shower," I lied. Dolan was passed out drunk. I knew I had to hang up soon. "Nolan?" I whispered.

"Yeah, sweets."

"Thanks for everything."

"Why do you say that like I'm not going to be a part of your life? We have kids to raise."

"What if they're not yours?"

"They'll still be mine."

"You're the best."

"I know," he laughed.

"I'll talk to you later."

"I hope it's soon," he said.

"Bye."

Dolan

I was trying my best to get home, but the bitch had locked me in my own office and refused to give up the key. At first, I didn't know what she was getting out of it until she tried to blackmail me into giving her money.

"If you don't pay me as promised for my services, I'll tell Darica."

"I never asked your bitch ass for your piss-poor sloppy-toppy anyway. *You* were the one who insisted on slobbering all over me. You need to call my wife to give you lessons because the shit you're doing is not hitting on nothing."

"Then I'll file a sexual harassment case against you. You're full of shit. I can't live on what you pay me to wait tables, so you need to pay up."

"Bitch, you're lucky to get what you got—my seeds in your mouth and a few extra dollars in your paycheck. As much as you drop the dishes, I ought to charge your ass for damages. I'll tell you what, though. I'll give you a thousand bucks. That's all my wife gave me today."

"That's some bullshit, Dolan. Pay me my money, or I'll call your wife."

"Good luck. She's mad at me, and she doesn't answer unknown numbers."

"I guess I'll have to show up over at your house."

"Let's see if you get past our alarm system, and if you do, you have an ass whooping coming from my wife. I don't control the money, so I don't see the point in you holding me up."

Darica had started handling the finances, and it wasn't like I was going to call her up and say, "Hey, baby, this bitch is due a couple of raises. Can you cut her a check?"

I had too much to drink and fell asleep a few times. By the time I woke up, it was well past three. When I woke up, the dumb broad was still standing there looking stupid as hell. I guess she ran out of options because she agreed to take the original offer. I gave her seven hundred and kept the other three in my pocket. By the time I got home, it was almost five in the morning, and it took me ten minutes to get my key in the door after I dropped them so many times and had to get on my knees and search for them. Darica was hot. I knew I didn't have too many more times to fuck up, and I was ashamed to face her, so I took my ass to the guest room and slept it off. A few hours later, Darica threw some cold water on me, and I pissed in the bed. I got up, threw up, and took a shower. By ten in the morning, I was feeling better and ready to talk to my wife.

"I don't want to fight no more, baby," I told her. "I'll get help." She slapped me three times, hugged me, and cried tears of joy.

"Thanks for coming with me," Miko sang. She looked happier than a kid in a candy store.

"My pleasure. I would've done it sooner, but I had to get my ducks in a row. I almost lost Darica over some dumb shit."

"I know the feeling. My guy was ready to give me my walking papers because I was avoiding him. You don't want to lose a good thing, especially when you work so hard to get it."

"You're right. That woman loved the ground I walked on, and all I gave her was my ass to kiss. I started going to AA meetings, and they seem to be working out. I go into rehab next month. I'm on a wait list, but a friend of a friend pulled some strings."

"*That's* what's up." She smiled as she grabbed my hand and walked into Dr. Ross's office.

"Hello, Dolan. You're looking radiant today."

"Do you mind if I tell her?" Miko asked.

"Not at all," I said. Miko brought Doc Ross up to speed about my reunion with Darica and my new endeavors.

"That's wonderful news," said Dr. Ross. "I'm so happy for you. If you need me for anything, please don't hesitate to ask."

"That's a plan," I said. "Now, what's going on with you that I had to be kept in suspense forever?" I asked Miko. She sighed, lay on the good doctor's chaise lounge, and relayed her story to me.

Miko said, "When I first laid eyes on you in high school, I knew you were meant to be mine. I pointed you out to Carlena, who was my best friend at the time, and she acted like I was crazy for having feelings for you. She was always making jokes about how atrocious I was, how I couldn't dress, and how I didn't know what to do with my hair. She said I was too immature for high school, my grammar sucked, and someone like you would never be interested in me, but I didn't take her seriously. I always thought she was just jealous because she didn't spot you first, and I, unfortunately, learned the hard way how right I was. If I'd known then what I know now, I never would've shared my innermost thoughts and secrets with her, and I damn sure wouldn't have done anything to make you hate me. I remember the conversation that led to our demise like it was yesterday. It was the very last day I loved Carlena as a sister."

***

"I saw Dolan today," I gushed to Carlena as we walked out of our summer school class.

"That's nice," she answered nonchalantly.

"He told me he has the house to himself all summer while his parents are at work."

"Did he invite you over?"

"No."

"Well, there you go. If he wanted to be bothered, he would've rolled out the red carpet for you."

"Well, actually, I invited myself."

"What?" she answered in disbelief. "Why would you do that? He's going to think you're desperate now."

"I don't care," I answered defiantly, determined not to let anything stand in my way.

"Don't snap at me. I'm just trying to help you. Men don't like women that give it up so easy. I think they call them chickenheads."

"Dolan's not like that. Besides, he and I are just friends; he knows I'm a virgin, so I don't think he'll judge me that harshly."

"Wait. You told him you're a virgin?"

"Yes. We're open with each other."

"Your stupid ass fell for that?"

"Fell for what?"

"Guys do that all the time to trick you into giving it up to them."

"Dolan wouldn't do that. He's a nice guy."

"Until he gets what he wants."

"What do you mean?"

"He probably bet all his friends he'd get in your thong first."

"Thong?"

"Never mind," she told me. She knew I didn't know what a thong was. I was still wearing briefs.

"I know a lot of guys that are virgins, and most of them are more scared to lose their virginity than girls."

"Okay, Mrs. Sexpert, you keep dreaming," she spat.

I didn't say anything after that. I just rolled my eyes and stomped away. I had an attitude the size of Texas. I'd told her a lot of details about an upcoming date Dolan and I had planned. She knew he was going over to Trent's house that day, and all of them would meet up with each other.

"I found out a secret about Dolan," she told me.

"What is it?"

"Well, I heard from a friend of a friend of his that Dolan is a voyeur."

"A what?"

"A person that likes to watch other people get down."

"Get down from what?"

"Pay attention, little girl, because I'm only going to say this once. Your crush has wild sexual fantasies."

"You must've heard wrong. I told you he's a virgin."

"I know some virgins that are kinky as hell."

"I don't follow you."

"Look, if you want to get your man, you need to grow up. Act like a tenth-grader for a change."

"What do I have to do?"

"Get over to Trent's house and seduce Nolan."

"What? I'm not trying to lose my innocence to Dolan's brother. That's insane."

"Girl, you need to quit with that act. I know you're not innocent. You let Ricky hit it a few weeks ago, and he told some of his friends. I killed the rumor for you by reminding everybody what a habitual liar he is. I'm not asking you to have sex with Nolan. It just needs to look like you are. I know you want Dolan, but he's not going to make a move on you until he sees you humping his brother. That's *what turns him on*."

"I don't know about that, Cee."

"You love him, don't you?"

"Yeah, but—"

"Just do what I say, and Dolan will fall madly in love with you. He'll probably make love to you right then and there. You'll be his first, and you two will probably end up getting married."

"You really think so?"

"I know so. Go home and shower, then change out of those hideous clothes. Nobody wears socks anymore, and head over to Trent's house. As soon as Nolan drops his guard, jump him. Dolan will get turned on and pull you away from his brother, and you'll have your happy ending."

"You're sure about this?"

"Yes. I wouldn't steer you wrong. Go get your man, girl."

I followed Carlena's advice and went to Trent's house. She was right. Nolan and I ended up talking up a storm. We hit it off so good you would've thought we knew each other long before then. Somehow, Nolan ended up asleep in Trent's guest room, and that's when I put my plan into action. One thing led to another, and our hormones took over. When you came in and saw us, not only did you not pull me off Nolan, you made a beeline for the nearest exit and left us to our own devices. The rest, as they say, was history.

"I tried to explain, but you treated me like the plague, and Nolan didn't want anything to do with me either. Carlena made sure she was there to lend you a shoulder to cry on, and after that, you were proud to let her be the first girl you made love to. I cried my eyes out for weeks and ended up hating her guts, but she didn't care because she had my man."

Dolan

Hearing how Carlena duped Miko into going over to Trent's house and doing the craziest stunt she ever pulled, all in the name of love, made me feel some type of way. If she hadn't done that, we would've gone out, painted the town, and probably had a wonderful relationship. Maybe she would've told me about her assault, and I would've given Ricky the ass whooping he deserved. Miko cried a river on my shoulder as she told me the details of that crazy day. I felt so bad for her; I wanted to wring Carlena's neck.

"I think she tried to kill your wife," Miko added.

"What! Darica and I have had some issues, but I don't think she would keep something like that from me."

"I think you all need to talk about it," Dr. Ross suggested.

"You're right," Miko agreed. "I'll tell you what I know when we get in the car," she promised.

I nodded, thanked Dr. Ross, and escorted Miko out of her office.

Darica called to tell me that April and Nuni planned to take her out. She deserved it after all the shit I put her through and after dealing with her difficult pregnancy. I promised her I wasn't going to touch a drink, and I hadn't, but I knew soon I would be getting some help, and since she wasn't home, I figured I could have a little taste and have plenty of time to sober up before she got back. I had a lot on my mind, including what Miko and I talked about in the car. If Carlena was the one who assaulted Darica, and Darica didn't tell me, she had a lot of explaining to do.

The next thing I knew, I'd finished a whole bottle and was on to my next. I marveled at how advanced I had become, polishing off ten times more than the average drinker. I almost fell as I walked to the bathroom to pee, and I think I passed out a few times. When I came to, it was almost nine o'clock, and I started to worry about my wife. She hadn't called me, even though she knew I warned her all the time how dangerous it was for a woman in her stage of pregnancy to not check in.

I jumped when my phone rang and smiled because I felt my wife heard my pleas for her to contact me. The caller ID showed up unknown, and I started not to answer; then I changed my mind. What if she'd gone into labor? I would never forgive myself if I weren't there for the delivery.

"Hello."

"Do you know where your wife is?" the caller asked. It was clear that it was a woman changing her voice to sound masculine.

"Who is this?"

"It's not important."

"What do you want?"

"I want to give you a heads-up."

"I'm waiting."

"She's at Sweets and Karaoke."

"That's nice. She's entitled to a little fun in her life."

"I guess you like sharing her with your brother."

I hung up the phone, grabbed my keys, and darted out of the house. Only God knows how I got downtown so fast, but the next thing I knew, I was on the off-ramp on Sutter Street and making my way into the S&K parking lot. All I cared about at this moment was getting my wife from my brother. That fucker thought he was slick, convincing my wife to lie to me so he could spend time with her. I distinctly told her ass that she was not to see my brother if she wanted me to do whatever she wanted and make this marriage work. It meant everything to me, and I was determined that they weren't going to fuck it up again.

Chapter Seventeen

Darica

It seemed like everybody and their mama was talking about S&K. Nolan and I thought we had a secret obsession when we started eating the sweet confection, the decadent chili cheese fries, and enjoying the cool, crazy contest that had everyone going insane for a chance to win money to act a fool. It had become one of the things that my friends wanted to conquer. Chevette, April, and Nuni cooed with delight as they signed their names to sing in the contest.

"Are you going to sing 'Sweet Thing'?" I asked Nuni.

"I'll probably sing a regular song."

"His ass is scary," April said.

"Girlfriend, I may be a lot of things, but scary I am not."

"I'm going to win the contest," April said.

"I don't know how, since you can't sing a lick," Chevette told her.

"I can sing better than you."

"I'll sing, but I don't know about if I want to enter the contest," said Chevette.

"Suit yourself. I'm winning that money," April said. They all ended up signing up and were eventually numbered as five, seven, and nine on the list. As we sat down to enjoy our shared ice cream and fries, I saw Nolan walk in and wondered if he knew I was coming here tonight. We locked eyes, I waved him over, and he smiled, grabbed the seat next to me, and quickly dipped into the food. One thing about S&K, they gave large portions.

The next thing I knew, Dolan came barreling into the restaurant. He looked mad as hell, and I could tell he was drunk. When he did manage to stagger over to us, we could barely make out what he was saying.

"Son ofa bitch." He pointed his finger at Nolan. "Why'n the hell you have my wife meet you here?"

Before anyone could say anything, Dolan grabbed him by the collar and shook the hell out of him.

"Man, let me go," Nolan said. "I didn't meet her here. I came here by myself. They were already here."

"Bullshit," Dolan said. "You wan my wife, and you'll do anything to get her, e'en put her own friends up to helping you. You guys ought to be shame of yourselfs. You see me and my wife tryna work it out, and ya over-over here infiltrating."

"The word is 'instigating,' stupid," April corrected him.

"You know what the fuck I mean."

"Hold up, wait a minute. Let me put some sugar in it," Nuni said. "Don't let the smooth taste fool you. I will whoop your drunk ass all over this restaurant."

Dolan let Nolan's collar go and centered his attention on me.

"Let's just go, Darica."

"No. I came here to have a good time, and that's exactly what I plan to do. You're drunk; you need to sit down somewhere."

"I'm not sitting down. I'm taking you home."

"Over my dead body," April said. "You can't even walk straight, let alone drive a car."

"I don't give a fuuuuck. She's c-c-coming wiff me. Let's go, Darica," he said. He began pulling my arm, yanking me out of the restaurant.

"Is everything okay?" the security guard asked.

"Get the fuck out of our business. We don't need your RoboCop-looking ass over here asking questions. I'm try-na take my wife home. Is zat a crime? Is zat okay witchu?"

"Dolan, why don't you calm down? No need to do all that cursing. You're making a scene," Chevette said.

"If her ass would get up and come on out to the car, I wouldn't have to do this. It's clear she came here to meet up with him. He won't get ta fuck her tonight."

"What kind of sense do you make?" April said. "She's pregnant with twins and can't even walk straight. How's she going to have sex with anybody?"

"Come on, Every," he ignored her and said, as he pulled me toward the exit. I wiped the newly formed tears out of my eyes and got up to walk away with him.

"Sweets, are you insane? My brother is drunk. He needs to sit it out. Go home with April. I'll bring him home."

"I told you, your motherfucking ass ain't my brother. Stop calling her sweetie. She don't take orders from you. I ain't riding witchu."

"Come on, man."

"I don't need you to take me nowhere." He jerked away from Nolan and almost fell.

"I'm just trying to help you, man. You can't drive."

"Read my lips, man," he said as he spit the words in Nolan's face and pushed his index finger in his chest. "You're *not* my fucking brother, and you're *not* getting my wife. Now, let's go, Darica."

To keep the peace, I got up and walked away with my husband. I offered to drive, but he wasn't having it. I prayed and kissed my cross as I let him drive out of the parking area and on to the freeway.

"So, this the damn thanks I get, huh?"

"Dolan, stop cursing."

"Don't tell me ta stop fucking cursing. I tried ta let you have a good time, and I find you in a restaurant eating with *him*."

"It's not what you think, baby. We were all just having a good time when Nolan came in."

"Let's see what he does when we move."

"Move?"

"Yes, I can't take this shit no more. We need to distance ourselves from Nolan and start over."

"I'm not moving away from my family, my friends, and the people I love."

"Then I guess you don't fucking love me."

"I love you more than anything. You're my everything, but I'm not going to let you fuck up my life."

"Like you fucked up mine?"

"You did a good job of that all by your damn self. You didn't need me or anybody else. You're always drunk and forever pointing the finger."

"Okay, well, let's see how much shit you talk in another state. As soon as we get home, get to packing your shit cuz we're out of here."

I stared at Dolan in disbelief. It was then that I realized that he was doing ninety on the freeway and barely staying in his lane. I prayed we would get pulled over before he crashed into something.

"Slow down, honey. I'll do anything you say."

"I know you will. You're going to listen to me. I'm going to be the man in this relationship from now on."

"Okay, honey, but slow down a little bit; you're scaring me."

"Is this fucker following us?" he said as he looked in his rearview mirror. I looked behind us, and sure enough, Nolan was a few cars away. I wanted to lie, but how many people drove a candy-apple red Ferrari?

"He's probably just trying to make sure we get home okay."

"Sure. Go 'head and cover for him. It's going to be a different story when we leave town."

"Why don't you pull over and let me drive?"

"No." He pushed the car harder, accelerating to ninety again. There was only a mile to go until we reached our off-ramp. I tried to sneak my phone so that I could text Nolan to tell him to back off.

"Don't fucking call him."

"I'm not calling him."

"Don't lie to me, Darica. You can kiss his ass goodbye because this the last time you gonna see him," Dolan said as he looked up just in time to see the exit. He managed to slow down and take the ramp, but when he went to make a right at the light, he turned into the opposing lane and crashed head-on into a big rig.

We bounced off it, flew off into another direction, and tumbled over, I don't know how many times. I saw flashes of light, psychedelic beams, shards of glass, more light, upside-down structures, and finally . . . darkness. It was definitely lights out.

When I came to, I saw flashing lights, yellow tape, and men running out of a fire truck; heard sirens, screams, yells, and cries. I saw the crushed-up Lamborghini and wondered how I survived the wreck . . . then wondered if I actually did make it. A paramedic had a small flashlight in my eyes.

"Ma'am, can you see me?"

"Yes. Where's my husband."
"What's your name?"
"Darica. Where is he?"
"Where is who?"
"The driver."
"Sorry, lady. He's gone."

To Be Continued . . .